D1528330

There's a Cat Girl in My Cubicle!

Volume Two

Austin Beck

CONTENTS

CHAPTER 1

The dungeon in MMORPG, "Celestial Quests" was as haunting as it was menacing. My avatar, a formidable warrior, led the way, armed to the teeth with a gleaming sword and plate steel armor. Not far behind were Momo's character, a tall, slender elf mage, and Hana's avatar, a short, stocky dwarf rogue. Our headsets were alive with friendly chatter, laughter, and the occasional strategy discussion.

Suddenly, Hana's rogue began to stutter-step on my screen, freezing mid-stride then jerking forward awkwardly. "Hana," I began, trying to suppress my laughter, "Your rogue looks like she's performing a disco dance rather than sneaking around a dungeon."

"Hilarious, Kazuki!" Hana retorted, her voice crackling with static and thinly veiled annoyance. "Just remember, not all of us have fancy gaming rigs. Some of us are trying to defeat evil on a laptop older than my mom."

Momo's soft laughter chimed in through the headset, "Come on, Hana. You know that running 'Celestial Quests' on that ancient laptop is like trying to win an Equation One race on a tricycle."

"I can't help it if my character's got the moves, okay?" Hana replied, a touch of amusement softening her voice.

Unable to resist, I jumped back into the conversation, "Trust me, Hana, your dwarf is doing anything but moving smoothly. It's more like she's trying to swat invisible flies while running."

Hana groaned loudly, her avatar glitching and teleporting around the screen in a pixelated frenzy. "You guys are impossible! Maybe I should just knock your characters off a cliff with my teleporting dwarf, then you'll shut the hell up."

The conversation was cut short when our party was ambushed by a horde of gruesome goblins. I immediately guided my warrior to the frontlines, hacking and slashing while Momo's mage cast powerful spells. Amidst the chaos, Hana's rogue was a wild card, her glitching avatar creating a spectacle.

"Good gracious, Hana," Momo giggled, "Your rogue just tried to backstab a goblin... but it was actually a tree."

"And now she's attempting to vanish into thin air ...but she's just standing still, swinging at nothing," I added. "Your dwarf has some serious commitment to making us laugh."

"Shut up, both of you!" Hana growled, though I could hear the muffled laughter in her voice. "At least my character has personality, unlike your boring super-powered douchbags."

Once the last goblin fell, Momo suggested, "Hana, you really should consider upgrading your laptop. Maybe something that doesn't predate the founding of Silver City."

I chuckled, adding, "Yeah, maybe we could start a 'get Hana a new laptop' quest in the game. Reward: no more disco-dancing dwarf!"

Hana, Momo, and I had been losing ourselves in the MMORPG called "Celestial Quests" for the past couple of weeks. This game was a universe in itself, called "Elysium," filled with countless races and mythical creatures. We crafted our characters from a variety of options. You could be anything, from classic elves and dwarves to exotic celestial beings or wisps.

We picked different professions, dabbling in blacksmithing, enchanting, even herbology. We explored, crafted, traded, and battled together.

The game's beauty was unreal. The landscapes were stunning, from the tall, snowy mountains to the vibrant, bustling cities. The night sky in the game was filled with stars and celestial bodies that we could visit. Video games here were much more technologically impressive than back on Earth.

Battles required strategy and skill. Every decision counted. The thrill of victory after an intense boss fight was something else. "Celestial Quests" was more than a game for us. It was an adventure that brought us together, a world that let us escape from work, and a backdrop against which our relationship deepened.

Let's face it, having gamer cat girls as lovers was about as good as life could get.

Our digital alter egos traversed deeper into the labyrinthine dungeon of "Celestial Quests," the tension only broken by the constant stuttering of Hana's rogue. Momo, often the more practical one among us, finally broke her silence.

"Hana," she started, her tone suggesting she was about to impart some sage wisdom, "You need to stop fooling yourself that your laptop can run this game on ultra-high settings. Just adjust your settings to something more... realistic."

"What? And let my game look like it was created 200 years ago?" Hana retorted defiantly. "I want the full immersive experience. I want to see the shimmering scales of the dragons, the magical glow of your spells, Momo. Not some 2D cardboard cut-out version."

"Hana," I chimed in, my character drawing his sword as we ventured deeper into the dungeon, "Right now, all we see is your dwarf breakdancing while we're trying to fight off ogres and dragons. I don't think this was the immersive experience the developers had in mind."

In the middle of our discussion, Hana's character suddenly veered toward the edge of a cliff in the game, a clear consequence of her technical issues. Momo let out a gasp, her avatar quickly casting a futile protection spell in Hana's direction.

"Hana, watch out!" she cried out, but it was too late. Hana's rogue danced an awkward jig at the precipice before tumbling off. The 'Player Down' notification flashed across our screens.

"Hana," Momo sputtered, trying to stifle her laughter, "Did you just...did you just swan dive off the cliff?"

Hana grumbled in reply, "Well, I couldn't see it, could I? One moment I was right there with you guys, the next moment, my screen froze, and I was already airborne!"

"Ah, the perils of high-definition gaming," I teased, my own laughter now uncontrollable. "I guess your rogue mistook a cliff for a goblin. An easy mistake, given how high-definition everything is for you."

Hana didn't respond right away, and when she finally did, her voice carried a note of reluctant resignation. "Fine...you win. I'm turning down the graphics."

As soon as she made the change, Hana's character, now more blocky for her but significantly more responsive, sprang back to life in the game.

"Holy cow, Hana!" Momo exclaimed, her laughter barely subsiding. "Your character actually looks like a rogue now. Albeit one made from BLEGO building blocks, but still an improvement!"

I added my own observations, "And look at that! She moves in real time, too. I mean, sure, she looks like she's made of melting wax, but who cares as long as she's not moonwalking while we're in the middle of a fight."

"Oh, hush, both of you!" Hana retorted, a hint of a smile in her voice. "Just you wait. Now that I'm not 'breakdancing,' I'll show you what I'm really capable of!"

I couldn't resist one last tease, "Well, Hana, as long as your capabilities don't involve any more cliff diving, we're on board!"

Our dungeon delve was progressing smoothly - well, as smoothly as can be expected with Hana's rogue finally contributing to the team instead of dancing solo. The banter had settled down when a sudden thought hit me, an amusing thought that might add a dash of real-world spice to our virtual quest.

"Hey ladies," I began, putting on my most mischievous voice, "As the valiant knight in this brave trio, risking life and limb against the terrors of this dungeon, I have but one humble request..."

"What's that, Kazuki?" Hana cut in, her tone suggesting she already sensed a prank brewing.

"I find myself pondering," I continued, my smirk broadening, "What might my courageous cat girl companions be wearing in the safety of their abodes while I face the shadowy perils of this ominous underworld?"

There was a pause, before Momo's laughter echoed through the headset. "Oh, Kazuki, you're impossible," she chuckled, her laughter mingling with the background music of the game. "Alright, since our knight in shining armor has made such a gallant request, I shall satisfy his curiosity."

Her voice dropped to a sultry whisper that sent a small shiver down my spine. "I'm wrapped in my scarlet silk pajamas, the ones with the delicate lace trim. They're as soft as a kitten's fur, and they fit just right.

Oh yeah, no panties or a bra. Is that the kind of detail our brave knight hoped for?"

A mental image of Momo in her red, lacy silk PJs made me gulp, momentarily forgetting my in-game surroundings. Not to be outdone, Hana chimed in before I could formulate a response.

"Uh-uh, Momo. I won't let you be the only one enticing our daring knight," Hana teased, her tone playfully competitive. "Let me paint a picture for you, Kazuki. I'm decked out in a pair of navy-blue satin PJs, complete with a delicate white bow at the front. They may lack the fiery allure of Momo's outfit, but they have a certain elegant charm of their own. I have my thong panties on but no bra."

I let out a soft whistle, the image of Hana in her satin PJs pairing up with the earlier one of Momo in my mind. Both were tantalizing in their own unique way.

"Well, aren't we a glamorous bunch tonight?" I mused out loud. "Here I am in my mundane shorts and a plain white T-shirt, facing off against the pixelated horrors of this forsaken dungeon, while you two beauties are luxuriating in silk and satin. I must say, I feel rather underdressed."

My admission sent waves of laughter through the voice chat, brightening the dungeon's grim ambiance. Their amusement was contagious, and I found myself chuckling along. "Perhaps I should upgrade my gaming attire to match your high standards, ladies," I joked, picturing myself in a silken robe and feathered slippers.

As we settled into a brief moment of respite within the game, a stillness draped over our dungeon delve. Breaking the silence, Momo's voice crackled through my headset, teasing and tempting, "You know, Kazuki, it's still pretty early, only 11:00pm. You could always swap the safety of your apartment for our own little sanctuary and behold these glamorous PJs in person. I assure you, they're even better up close."

Her words hung in the air, stirring up an exciting whirl of images in my mind. The thrill of it, the prospect of leaving my solitary gaming station to join them in person was appealing, to say the least. It was a shift from our usual routine, an enticing twist to our shared evening. And as though her flirtatious invite wasn't enticing enough, Hana was quick to join the fray.

"Oh yes, Kazuki," Hana chimed in, her voice alive with anticipation, "Our brave knight could indeed embark on a real-life quest. If you dare to face the horrors of this forsaken dungeon, surely two cat girls adorned in silk and satin shouldn't be too intimidating, should they?"

Her words elicited a ripple of laughter from all of us, the sound ringing out, warm and inviting, amidst the eerie in-game ambiance. Their jesting, wrapped in flirtatious innuendo, hung tantalizingly in the virtual air between us.

There was an appealing allure to their invitation. As much as our virtual adventures were an escape from reality, the prospect of a real-world encounter was an enticing possibility. However, before I could respond, a horde of pixelated monsters charged at us, demanding our immediate attention. The virtual world, it seemed, wasn't ready to release its grip on us just yet. "Hold that thought, ladies," I managed to say, my focus shifting back to the onslaught of our digital adversaries. "Our brave knight has a duty to protect his damsels in distress, even if they're in silk and satin."

******

Walking up to Hana and Momo's apartment, I felt a peculiar sensation wash over me - a blend of anticipation, excitement, and a touch of nervousness. The friendly glow seeping from their windows seemed almost symbolic, a beacon signaling an unexpected adventure that lay just beyond the threshold. The apartment, our shared haven, was no longer just a familiar setting of many an after-work hangout. It had morphed into something far more significant - a testament to our evolving relationship.

Cradled in my hand, the key to their apartment felt heavier than it truly was. Its metallic coolness seemed almost out of place against my warm palm, a strange contrast much like our unusual relationship. They'd entrusted me with it a few days after our unforgettable night together. That small piece of metal was symbolic, an affirmation of their trust in me, of our collective decision to transition from mere colleagues to something profoundly more intimate.

Stepping into the quiet apartment, I was engulfed by its tranquil warmth. The hushed silence seemed almost like a blanket, comforting and welcoming, as if the walls themselves were welcoming me. The ambiance was serene, the only light coming from the dimmed lamps casting an enchanting glow around the rooms. It was a familiar place, filled with countless memories of laughter, shared meals, and now, shared intimacy.

"Hana? Momo?" I called out tentatively into the silence. My voice, slightly higher than usual, echoed around the apartment. I half-expected it to feel strange, this vocal admission of my presence. But, instead, it felt right, like the final piece of a jigsaw falling into place.

Their reply was almost immediate, the sound of their voices slicing through the still air, their lilt carrying a familiar, delightful warmth. "We're in here, Kazuki," came Hana's response, playful and flirtatious as always. Momo wasn't far behind, her tone imbued with a rich, teasing timbre. "Took you long enough, brave knight. Your damsels were starting to think you'd run off with a goblin princess."

I chuckled feeling a surge of affection. As I removed my shoes, placing them carefully by the door, Walking deeper into the apartment, their intertwined voices and shared laughter lingering in the air, I realized that

I was embarking on an entirely new quest. This was no digital dungeon filled with pixelated monsters; this was real life, with real feelings, and real consequences. The prospect was both exhilarating and intimidating. But then again, isn't that what every adventure is about?

As I nudged open the door to Hana's bedroom, time seemed to slow to an almost torturous pace. The sight that met my eyes was nothing short of breathtaking - an ethereal tableau etched into the soft lighting of the room that left me utterly spellbound. There they were - Hana and Momo, sprawled languidly on the bed, their bodies naked and utterly unashamed. A gasp escaped my lips, and I felt my jaw drop open, the shock of the sight hitting me like a punch.

Every line, every curve of their bodies was bared to my gaze - a stunning display of vulnerability and desire that rendered me breathless. My heartbeat quickened to a frenzied tempo, each throb echoing the pulsing desire that flooded my veins. A distinct stiffness overtook my lower body, a primal reaction to the raw sensuality displayed before me.

Hana, with her playful glint, broke the spellbinding silence, her voice smooth as honey. "Kazuki, so nice of you to come and save us from the horde of scary monsters," she teased, her lips curving into a smirk that held a wicked promise.

I swallowed, struggling to find my voice amidst the whirlwind of emotions swirling within me. "You two... you look... my god, you look amazing," I finally managed to stutter, my voice hoarse with the overwhelming surge of desire.

Momo's reaction was immediate and startlingly inviting. She spread her legs wider, revealing the intimate secret between her thighs. The sight of her shaven center stole my breath, a wave of hunger washing over me. "Are you hungry?" She questioned, her voice laced with an alluring tone that sent shivers down my spine.

"Umm, yeah," was all I managed to choke out, my hands reaching for the hem of my shirt. The fabric slid over my head with a swift motion, my body eagerly responding to the implicit invitation.

The words that left Momo's lips next were far from a mere suggestion - they were a direct order, a carnal command that sent my heart pounding in my chest. "Well, come here for a late night snack and eat my pussy."

In response, I fumbled with the fastening of my jeans, my fingers trembling with excitement and anticipation. I struggled to shed them, nearly stumbling and colliding with the dresser in my haste.

Hana, watching our exchange, let out a rich laugh, a sound that seemed to reverberate in the silence of the room. "I think Kazuki is excited," she commented, her fingers teasing her mocha nipples, her own excitement mirrored in her actions. The combination of her words and her actions sent a fresh wave of arousal coursing through me, setting the stage for the night of shared passion that was yet to unfold.

I dipped my head lower, my lips gently gracing the soft, sensitive skin of Momo's inner thigh. The tender contact ignited a sharp intake of breath from her, the sensual sound whispering promises of the pleasure that awaited her. Her muscles tensed in sweet anticipation, her body yearning for the intimate caress of my lips upon her intimate folds.

Meanwhile, Hana had propped herself up, her hazel eyes wide and entranced, her gaze unyielding as it followed the trail of my kisses on Momo's body. She was an enthralled audience, captivated by the explicit performance that unfolded before her. The sight of me hungrily indulging in Momo's intoxicating taste was nothing short of a carnal spectacle for her, and it was clear that it left her profoundly affected.

As my tongue made contact with Momo's glistening core, I was rewarded with a rush of her sweet essence. The taste was uniquely her, a complex mixture of arousal, warmth, and intimacy that caused an undeniable surge of desire in me. The sensation sent a tightening coil of heat spiraling through me, my arousal growing painfully hard.

Momo's voice rang out through the room, her words peppered with raw, uninhibited pleasure. "Kazuki, uh, that's so good... Don't stop... Holy fuck," she panted out. Her words, laced with desire, were a testament to the pleasure coursing through her body, an affirmation of the ecstasy I was delivering.

My hands sought out the curves of her body, fingers finding the soft mounds of her breasts. The feeling of her ample flesh beneath my palms was electric, each caress met with a gasp or a whimper from Momo. She responded to my touch instinctively, arching her back and pushing her hips upward, pressing her dripping wet sex further into my face. Her fingers threaded through my hair, pulling me closer, a silent plea for more of my undivided attention.

Meanwhile, Hana was not merely a passive observer. Her breath hitched audibly, the sound cutting through the heavy silence. "Damn, this is fucking hot," she murmured, her voice thick with desire. Her hand snaked its way down her body, disappearing between her thighs. The unmistakable, wet sound of her fingers exploring her own heated folds only served to fuel the erotic atmosphere in the room.

As Momo's breaths came in short, sharp gasps, her body started to tremble beneath me. "Goddamn, I'm going to come... Don't stop, you make me feel so good," she breathed out, her voice barely more than a desperate whimper. Her body was a testament to the pleasure consuming her, each shudder, each moan echoing the impending climax threatening to unravel her.

Answering her silent plea, my fingers found her hardened nipples, pinching and tweaking them to add another layer to the sensory overload she was experiencing. Her reaction was immediate and intense, her body arching off the bed as a loud cry tore from her throat. The explosive rush of her climax hit her, her body convulsing in the throes of pleasure. The flood of her warmth filled my mouth, a sweet testament to the shared ecstasy we had just experienced.

A triumphant grin adorned Hana's face as she declared her intentions. "My turn!" She announced, her voice dripping with unmasked anticipation. There was a certain glimmer in her hazel eyes, one that promised a shared intimacy that went beyond just physical pleasure.

I moved my focus toward her, studying the woman laid bare before me. "What do you want, Hana?" I questioned, my voice low and charged. My fingers traced the smooth expanse of her stomach, inching lower, stopping just before her heated core.

With an air of unashamed desire, she gazed back at me, her reply carrying the weight of her longing. "I want that big cock in my pussy. Can you do that for me, Kazuki?" The words were like a promise, a carnal pact forged between us.

The corners of my mouth lifted in a wicked grin, as my erection teased her wet folds. A simple touch, yet it caused a sharp intake of breath from her. "You want me to be gentle, or do you want me to be a savage?" I asked, my tone deliberately provocative.

Her laugh, a soft giggle, filled the room, as she bit her bottom lip in anticipation. The sight of her cat incisors protruding only added to her seductive allure. "I want savage Kazuki," she requested, her voice daring me to fulfill her request.

From the corner of my eye, I could see Momo. The green-haired cat girl had recovered from her climax and was reveling in the sexual tension that hung heavy in the room. "Ooo, savage Kazuki sounds fun," she chimed in, her voice laced with lust.

Answering Hana's challenge, I guided myself into her, sinking deeply into her tight warmth. I could feel her muscles clenching around me as I began to thrust into her. The raw intensity of the act drove us both to a frenzied pace. "You like that?" I asked, my voice a husky whisper.

Her reply was a moan-laced affirmation. "Fuck yeah," she gasped, her nails digging into my shoulders.

With every thrust, her breasts swayed enticingly. Hana's breasts were a sight to behold, not as large as Momo's, but every bit as enticing. Each bounce was like an erotic dance, mesmerizing me and fueling my desire for her.

Her tightness was intoxicating, each thrust eliciting a moan from her lips. "Damn, you're so tight. Do you want me to loosen up your little pussy?" I groaned, my words filled with a potent mixture of lust and adoration.

"Yes, fuck!" She cried out, her voice hitched, her body moving in rhythm with my thrusts.

Meanwhile, Momo was far from idle. Her playful voice floated over to us. "I think you're going to break my best friend," she teased, her hand disappearing between her own thighs.

A brow arched in response. "And what exactly are you doing over there, Momo?" I prodded, a lopsided grin on my face.

She shot me a teasing glance, her green eyes dancing with amusement. "What does it look like? I'm mas-

turbating while I watch you fuck. Best show in town,"
she retorted playfully, her words filling the room with
a contagious, sensual energy.

Hana's voice came out in desperate pleas, each
one echoing my own spiraling desire. "I'm gonna
come, Kazuki. Don't stop," she demanded, her words
were urgent, filled with unbridled anticipation. Her
brown eyes locked onto mine, communicating a fervent promise of shared ecstasy.

The ensuing moments were a blur, a euphoric haze
that seemed to consume all reason. The soft gasps and
cries that escaped Hana transformed into unabashed
screams of pleasure. The force of her release caused the
picture frames lining the bedroom walls to tremble,
their occupants dancing to the rhythm of her climax.

The sight of her, a beautiful cat girl writhing beneath me, consumed by the pleasure I was giving her,
was overwhelmingly erotic. The sheer intensity of it
caused an unmistakable tightening in my balls, an undeniable sign of my impending climax.

At that moment, I felt Momo's hot breath ghosting
over my ear, her soft, seductive whispers filling the
air. "Looks like you're going to come in her," she said,

her voice tinged with a hint of excitement. She gently bit down on my earlobe, the sudden jolt of sensation causing a shiver to run down my spine.

Caught in the wave of passion, I managed to voice a husky question to Hana. "Do you want my seed inside you?" The question hung heavy in the air, a potent mixture of lust and anticipation undeniable between us.

Momo, always the playful one, interjected with a saucy offer. "If she doesn't, I sure do," she announced, her tone daring, a smirk playing on her lips.

Yet Hana had her answer ready, her voice breathless and filled with desire. "Yes, I want you to fill me up. Paint my pussy and make me yours." Her words were an open invitation, a pledge of surrender.

Driven by her words, I plunged into her with renewed vigor. The bed shook with the intensity of our joining. Each thrust brought me closer to the edge until finally, I reached it. The world narrowed as my cock pulsed, releasing white ropes of cum deep inside of Hana.

As the pleasure began to subside, the reality of my situation began to settle in. I had two cat girl lovers.

Two stunningly beautiful, unique individuals who had chosen to share their love and their bodies with me. The realization was both mind-boggling and incredibly humbling. The simple fact that I was lying in bed with two cat girls continued to amaze me.

CHAPTER 2

Saturday morning arrived, a blessed break in our office routine, and this one was filled with the warmth of the summer sun and an air of anticipation. Momo and I had schemed a special surprise for Hana, our companion in love and life. We'd seen her gritting her teeth and grinding through her games on an antiquated laptop that stuttered and lagged far too much for any gamer's peace of mind. We knew it was time for an upgrade, and not just a small one. Hana deserved nothing but the best, and Momo and I were more than eager to give it to her. Rebecca my dedicated AI assistant had helped me with investments. Part of her duties at my apartment was to watch the stock market and make me money. She was shockingly good at it. I had begun to build a nice nest egg of money. I couldn't think of a better way to use this excess of money than helping my girlfriends. I couldn't wait to see Hana's face when we presented her with a beast of a machine.

As the Whisker Wonders Consulting's IT whiz, Momo was my partner in crime for this mission. She wore her love for gaming as a badge of honor, and her tech-savvy mind would be the key to unlocking the best gaming rig for Hana. Between her eye for good hardware and her understanding of Hana's needs, I was confident we would find the perfect match.

I had received a notification from my AI assistant, Rebecca. She had scoured every nook and cranny of the digital world to pinpoint the perfect store for our mission in Silver City. The marvels of AI research never failed to impress me, and this was no exception.

The message from Rebecca suggested a renowned electronics store - 'Great Purchase'. "Momo, Rebecca says Great Purchase has the best selection for gaming laptops," I relayed the information to Momo, watching her face light up at the news.

"Great Purchase, huh?" She grinned, her sharp canines making a quick appearance. "Sounds like a good start."

We hailed a taxi, quickly getting absorbed in the bustling cityscape of Silver City. Settling into the backseat, I turned to Momo, her eyes gleaming with the day's promise. "This is going to be fun, don't you think?"

"Yeah," she replied, a mischievous glint in her eyes. "Shopping, gaming, and surprising Hana - the perfect combination."

This wasn't just a simple shopping expedition. This was a quest, an adventure, and a shared secret that brought Momo and me closer. As the taxi whisked us toward Great Purchase, we chatted about potential models and features, analyzing and hypothesizing.

"Remember, Hana likes a sleek design," Momo said, her brow furrowed in thought. "But she also needs power and speed for her games."

"I know, I know," I laughed, recalling the countless times Hana had ranted about her laptop's poor performance. "And we need something sturdy too. You know how she gets during intense gaming sessions."

I began to picture Hana's face when we'd reveal the surprise. The way her brown eyes would widen in delight, her surprised gasp followed by that unique, heart-warming laugh of hers. I shared my musings with Momo, and we found ourselves laughing and looking forward to our girlfriend's reaction.

We left the cab, standing before the massive facade of Great Purchase. The Great Purchase was a monolith of technology and innovation, standing proudly amidst the hustle and bustle of Silver City. Its grand exterior gave off an air of sleek modernity, matching the cutting-edge gadgets housed within. The facade was a polished array of glass and steel.

As we approached, our eyes were drawn to the massive LED display screens that covered the entrance, showcasing a dazzling array of high-definition graphics. Flashing advertisements, product reviews, and promotional videos danced across the screens, drawing the attention of passersby. The store's logo, a bold 'Great Purchase', shone brightly above the doors, its sleek silver letters a beacon of promise to all tech enthusiasts.

As we stepped through the automatic sliding doors, we were greeted by the hum of electricity, the soft glow of countless electronic displays, and the faint scent of new tech. The store was like a labyrinth of electronic wonders, with rows upon rows of shelves stocked to the brim with the latest technology. Each aisle was clearly labeled, guiding customers to their desired products — computers, gaming consoles, home appliances, mobile phones, audio equipment, and more.

The air was filled with a low murmur of excited chatter from fellow customers, punctuated by the occasional beeping of barcode scanners at the checkout counters. A soft, unobtrusive electronic melody played in the background, adding to the store's ambiance.

In one corner, there was a spacious section dedicated solely to computers. Sleek desktop towers, high-performance gaming rigs, versatile laptops — it was a haven for any computer enthusiast. I could see several customers already there, engrossed in testing keyboards and scrutinizing spec sheets.

Above us, suspended from the high ceiling, were screens displaying customer reviews, staff recommendations, and tech news updates. This was the Great Purchase experience — not just a store, but a celebration of technology, a symphony of sounds, sights, and sensations. It was a hub of discovery, innovation, and, of course, great purchases we hoped at least.

Stepping into the labyrinthine world of the laptop aisle felt akin to crossing a threshold into a realm where technology reigned supreme. The towering shelves on both sides represented the evolution of portable computing – a living museum of human ingenuity and innovation. This aisle was a testament to the insatiable march of technology; a microcosm that told the story of humankind's ceaseless quest for power, speed, and mobility.

On the shelves closest to us lay the simpler, more modest specimens. The "NetSpry" series – compact, lightweight, economical. Perfect for students and casual users looking for efficient internet browsing and light office work. These little workhorses were the everyman's choice, offering reliable, straightforward computing for those who didn't require frills.

Venturing deeper, we encountered the "TechRoar" line-up – a step up from the basic NetSpry range.

They promised more power, more versatility, more bang for your buck. With their sleek design and solid hardware, these machines were the choice of many professionals, capable of multitasking like a seasoned juggler at a circus.

As our eyes drifted further along the shelves, the "UltraPulse" models caught our attention. They were the middle children of the laptop world – offering the perfect blend of performance and price. More refined and powerful than the TechRoar laptops, they were favored by casual gamers and professionals who needed a machine as flexible as they were.

Next in the procession were the premium "Power-Dynamics" ultrabooks. Slick, stylish, and ultra-powerful, these devices were an embodiment of a digital nomad's dream. With their high-resolution, anti-glare displays, impressive battery life, and processors that shrugged off intense workloads with relative ease, they were the preferred choice of those who liked their laptops like they liked their coffee - strong and capable.

Finally, at the far end of the aisle, sat the veritable titans of the laptop world. The gaming powerhouses. First, the "PhantomStrike" series – aggressive and striking with its sharp lines and customizable RGB lighting. They were beasts, designed with the singular goal of elevating the gaming experience. High-refresh-rate screens, top-tier processors, graphics cards that scoffed at the term 'overkill', and an aesthetic that screamed 'gamer' – these machines had it all.

Adjacent to them sat the unrivaled champions, the "TitanForge" series. Here was the absolute pinnacle of portable gaming. The most powerful processors available, the cream of the crop when it came to graphics cards, RAM that could shame many desktops, and cooling solutions that could probably handle a small volcano. These were machines that knew no compromise, made for those who demanded the best.

As we stood in awe of these monstrous machines, a gruff voice pulled us out of our reverie. Turning, we found ourselves face to face with the most unlikely of sales associates. A dwarf with the name Thoren on his name tag, sporting a standard issue Great Purchase polo shirt. His rough hands, callused from years of what looked like hard labor, moved with practiced ease over the keys and screens of the laptops.

"Aye, ye be lookin' for somethin'?" He rumbled, his voice echoing tales of mountain halls and blazing forges. We shared our mission – to find the perfect gaming powerhouse to surprise our friend. His eyes twinkled with interest as he rolled his fingers over his coarse beard, his mind already ticking over the options.

"Well, laddie and lassie, ye came to the right dwarf. Let's see what we can do for ye, shall we?" He led us through the labyrinth of deals, discounts, and features – explaining the strengths and weaknesses of each model with a keen understanding. It was as if the dwarf had forged these machines himself, such was his familiarity with their intricate specifications. It was a strange encounter, but in the world of technology, who were we to question a dwarf's love for electronics?

Momo's fingers danced on the surface of the PhantomStrike she had been evaluating. "Well Kazuki, if we're talking the best brands, it's going to be PhantomStrike or TitanForge," she stated firmly, glancing at me from the corner of her eye. "The TitanForces are the absolute top-tier though, unmatched in power but with a price tag to match. Remember, this isn't corporate money we're spending - it's yours."

Her words carried a serious tone, but I understood her concern. Still, I had already decided. Hana had suffered her decrepit old machine for far too long. "She's stuck by that ancient machine far longer than most people would have," I countered, staring down the lit-up displays with a new determination. "Let's get her something that does justice to her gaming skills. She deserves that much."

Having made up my mind, I turned to our unlikely electronics sales associate. "Thoren, can you show us the most powerful TitanForge laptop you have in stock?"

The gruff dwarf's eyes twinkled, as if our request sparked a fire in his fantasy-filled heart. "Aye, ye've got good taste, laddie," he praised, leading us deeper into the laptop section of the store. We stopped before an imposing machine encased in a shining glass display.

"Feast yer eyes on this, the TitanForge Pinnacle-X," he announced with a theatrical flourish. His voice held a note of reverence. "This beauty ain't just a laptop, it's a promise - a promise that no game or software is too great a challenge."

With that, Thoren began detailing the specs. "At the very core of this behemoth rests the latest Octacore TitanEngine-X processor. A powerhouse designed to deliver unrivaled performance, no matter the task at hand. Pair that with a mind-blowing 64 gigabytes of the fastest HyperBlitz RAM available on the market, and ye've got a machine that scoffs at the concept of multitasking."

My eyes widened in awe. "That's... that's even more powerful than my desktop rig," I admitted.

Undeterred, Thoren continued his animated rundown. "We're just scratchin' the surface, lad. The Pinnacle-X is equipped with the groundbreaking PhantomX 5000 series graphics card. Whether it's the latest MMORPG or a graphics-intensive design software, this beast can handle it with ease."

As Thoren enthusiastically listed the features, Momo leaned in, her voice barely above a whisper. "Kazuki, this machine is an absolute monster. Hana will probably faint when she sees it."

"That's the plan," I replied, grinning as the rugged dwarf soldiered on with his introduction.

"Storage ain't a concern here either," Thoren assured us. "The Pinnacle-X boasts a 2 terabyte SSD - that's instant load times and ample space for all yer large game files. Plus, a state-of-the-art cooling system with AeroVane technology that'll keep the machine cool even during the most intense gaming sessions."

With his arms folded over his chest, Thoren finished his monologue. "In short, this TitanForge ain't just the mightiest laptop in our store. It's likely the best ye'll find anywhere in Silver City."

After a moment of silence, Thoren added, "The price, however, reflects its capabilities. The Pinnacle-X is 5,000 credits."

There was a pause as Momo looked at me, the question in her eyes. I nodded, undeterred by the price. "Momo," I said, a determined edge in my voice, "I think we've found Hana's new battle station."

"Five thousand credits? No way!" Momo exclaimed, her eyes going wide as saucers. She had a playful pout on her face, an attempt to conceal her surprise at the hefty price. "That's like...a bajillion dinners at that fancy sushi place you love."

I simply shrugged in response, a hint of a smirk playing on my lips. "Well, let's just say the stock market and I have been on quite the winning streak. I reckon it's about time I treated Hana to something special."

Momo's jaw practically hit the floor at my nonchalance. Her hands flew to her hips, her eyebrows furrowing in mock indignation. "And what about me, huh? Do I get some of this newfound wealth showered on me too?"

I laughed, the sound echoing through the laptop aisle. "Oh? And do you need a new gaming beast too? I thought your custom-built rig was your pride and joy."

She rolled her eyes at me and crossed her arms, a smirk tugging at her lips. "Ugh, you're so annoying. No, I don't need a new computer, dummy. I just need you to spend your credits on me too. Show a girl she's special, y'know?"

I raised an eyebrow, my gaze sweeping over the glittering aisles of the store. "Sure thing. So, what'll it be? New headphones, maybe a virtual reality set?"

Momo thought for a second, then broke into a fit of giggles. "Nah. Just grab me a soda, Kazuki. Then we're all square."

I leaned down to press a quick peck on her forehead. Her vibrant green hair brushed against my nose, causing a ticklish sensation. "You drive a hard bargain, Momo," I said, grinning widely. "Deal."

CHAPTER 3

We had just hailed a cab back to Hana and Momo's apartment after securing the surprise gift. The back-and-forth banter during the ride was punctuated by moments of silence, as the view of Silver City blurred past the cab window. Without Hana's lively presence, the apartment felt a bit empty when we finally arrived.

As I was turning the key in the front door, Momo looked over at me with a twinkle in her eye. "Kazuki, I've got a thought. How about we set up Hana's new laptop right here and now?"

I paused, the keys in my hand as I processed her suggestion. "So, we just... set everything up, get it all running, and leave it out for her?"

"Exactly!" Momo's eyes sparkled with amusement, her mischievous grin a clear indication of her anticipation. "And then when she gets back, we tell her there's a new update for 'League of Ancients,' the MOBA we've all been hooked on recently. It'd be hilarious to see her reaction."

I chuckled at the thought. Hana was usually sharp as a tack, but she might just be oblivious enough to start downloading a patch without noticing the new machine. "And you really think she won't realize it's not her usual rig?"

Momo shrugged, her smile still wide. "Well, she's been so engrossed in 'League of Ancients' recently. I wouldn't be surprised if she started the download without realizing she's not on her old laptop."

Laughing together at the thought, I had to admit, it sounded like a fun idea. "Alright, let's give it a shot. Let's get this setup going and give Hana a surprise she won't soon forget." With our plan set in motion, the once quiet apartment was now filled with the buzz of Hana's impending return.

As the clatter of plastic and the crinkle of paper came from the living room, I hefted the two bags of fresh ingredients onto the kitchen counter. The new laptop was being set up by Momo in the next room, and I had a culinary challenge of my own to tackle. Rebecca, my diligent AI assistant, had recently introduced me to an exciting new recipe - Spicy Miso Ramen with homemade chili oil. A dish that struck a delicate balance between fragrant spices and comfort food, a tantalizing challenge I was eager to master.

Momo, her eyes bright with curiosity and anticipation, poked her head into the kitchen, her hands covered in plastic wrapping from the new computer. "Are you really going to cook ramen from scratch, Kazuki? That's ambitious!" she teased, her eyes sparkling with excitement. Momo was a ramen aficionado, it was well-known among us.

I returned her grin, carefully beginning to unpack the ingredients and placing them neatly on the counter: Fresh ramen noodles, a package of ground pork, an assortment of vibrant vegetables, a tub of miso paste, a carton of chicken stock, and an army of exotic spices and condiments. "Yeah, Rebecca showed me this recipe," I told her, excitement bubbling within me as I looked over the ingredients. "If it turns out well, we might have a new favorite dish."

Leaning against the door frame, Momo folded her arms and watched as I washed my hands, ready to begin the cooking process. "You know, there's something undeniably sexy about a man who knows his way around a kitchen," she confessed, her lips curving into a teasing grin.

With a chuckle, I turned on the stove, heating up the pan. "Well, let's hope my cooking skills are as appealing as you think. Time to see if I can whip up a ramen that lives up to your expectations."

The kitchen quickly filled with the delicious aroma of cooking food. As the ground pork sizzled in the pan, it quickly transformed from a pink mass into a golden-brown delicacy. Adding the diced vegetables, I sautéed them until they were tender, their fresh scent blending with the cooked meat. The base of the ramen was coming together, and I felt a wave of satisfaction.

"Wow, it's smelling amazing in here, Kazuki!" Momo exclaimed, her eyes wide with surprise. "Are you sure you haven't secretly been a professional chef in your past life?"

Laughing at her playful jest, I began to carefully spoon the miso paste into the pan, stirring it into the mixture. "Well, you never know, Momo. I might just be a man of hidden talents! I did have a dream once that I was a powerful barbarian chef with insane cooking skills and big ass muscles."

As the minutes went by the aroma of the simmering ramen filled every corner of the apartment, blending beautifully with the quiet clatter of the keyboard as Momo set up the new laptop. Her excited commentary on the laptop's features, the sizzle of the cooking, and the growing anticipation for Hana's return created a rich tapestry of sounds and scents.

"Hey, Kazuki, just got a text from Hana. She's in a cab and will be here any minute," Momo announced, a note of anticipation evident in her voice. She'd been peeking through the blinds every now and then, eager for Hana's arrival and the revelation of our surprise.

"Perfect," I responded with a smile, my gaze turning from the simmering pot of ramen to the sight of our modest dining table. Its polished wooden surface seemed to beckon, ready to play host to the special meal I'd prepared.

As the rich aroma of ramen filled the room, I moved toward the cupboards, retrieving the three deep bowls we often used for our ramen dinners. They were simple, their off-white ceramic exteriors housing an array of deep blue and gold patterns inside. The mere sight of them already seemed to promise the comforting delight of the meal to come.

Next, I fetched the black lacquered chopsticks, their elegant simplicity contrasting beautifully with the vibrant bowls. Setting them down, I admired how their presence on the table began to shape the casual yet intimate dining setting we loved.

I didn't forget the spoons - the deep ones perfect for a hearty slurp of the ramen broth. I added them to the arrangement, completing each place setting with a spoon and pair of chopsticks. Now, the table was truly ready for the ramen - and for Hana's arrival.

Finally, I pulled out the condiments - a small dish of chili oil for an extra kick of heat, a jar of toasted sesame seeds for a nutty crunch, and a container of thinly sliced green onions for a burst of freshness. Each was laid out with care, their vivid colors and tantalizing aromas setting the stage for the ramen I was about to serve.

As I turned off the stove, a contented sigh escaping my lips, the aroma of the cooked ramen filled the apartment even more potently. The table was set, the meal prepared, and our surprise awaited Hana's return. I couldn't wait to see the look on her face.

The unmistakable sound of the apartment key turning the front lock filtered through the domestic ambience, heralding Hana's return. The door opened with a creak, revealing her lithe form, backlit by the fading twilight outside. She paused in the entrance, her delicate nostrils flaring slightly as they caught the enticing scent wafting through the air. "What in the world is that heavenly aroma?" She inquired, her voice echoing in the hall, full of a childish curiosity.

Slipping off her shoes at the entrance, she wandered further into the apartment, led by the intoxicating smell. "Seriously guys, my stomach is doing backflips. I am starving!" She confessed, her voice a mix of playful accusation and genuine hunger.

Making her way to the kitchen, her eyes fell upon the sight of me stirring a simmering pot, and a beautifully set table just waiting to host the imminent feast. A gasp slipped past her lips as her eyes grew wider with delight. "Oh wow, Kazuki, this is... impressive!" she complimented, her tone full of admiration.

I grinned at her, trying to seem modest yet obviously pleased at her reaction. "I thought I'd venture into a new culinary territory," I confessed, using the ladle to stir the broth in a circular motion.

Momo, who had been lounging on the couch, perked up at Hana's entrance and comments. Joining her friend at the kitchen entrance, she peeked over Hana's shoulder at the bowls of ramen. "See what happens when we let Kazuki in the kitchen? We need to do this more often," she quipped, her tone playful yet laced with a layer of sincerity.

Hana responded with a bright laugh, the sound echoing in the small space, adding to the homely ambience. She gently nudged Momo's shoulder, her brown eyes sparkling with amusement. "Seriously, Momo! If this is the result, maybe I should consider leaving the apartment more often!"

Momo, who was always full of energy and vivacity, slurped a noodle rather ungracefully. Her action was reminiscent of a cat grooming itself, and she completed the spectacle with an exaggerated smack of her lips. Setting her chopsticks down, she shifted her mischievous gaze toward Hana.

"Hana, darling, give us the gossip!" she playfully commanded, her chin resting on one hand while the other waved around for emphasis. "You can't keep us in suspense. How was your little voyage to the mothership?" Her chuckling filled the room, and it was contagious.

Hana let out a sigh and reclined into her chair. The way she rolled her eyes was almost melodramatic, but her smirk suggested she was more amused than truly bothered. "Oh, you know how Mom is," she began, that smirk never leaving her face, "She's flying high in 'helicopter parent' mode. Overprotective is a gross understatement!"

At this, I chuckled, finding it easy to relate. It wasn't my own mother we were discussing, but the universal motherly instinct seemed to be quite similar across the board. "Isn't that just the eternal paradox of parenthood?" I interjected, my voice bouncing with amusement. "They envelop you with so much love and attention that it's almost suffocating, and even when you're on the brink of insanity, they won't let up."

Hana and Momo broke into a fit of laughter at this. Once the laughter had died down slightly, Hana continued, her voice striking a balance between amused and exasperated. "And, oh boy, you won't believe the icing on the cake this time!" She paused, letting the suspense build, before leaning in as if she was about to disclose a juicy secret. "She went all out interrogating me about my love life...again."

Momo lost it at this, her giggles erupting like a volcanic burst, filling the apartment with a contagious, light-hearted energy. "No way! The old 'find a nice man and settle down' narrative? She's still hung up on that?"

Hana nodded, feigning a deep sigh. "Yep, exactly that!" She confirmed, placing a hand over her heart in a theatrical manner. "I mean, if she even had a hint of our... 'unique' living situation," she said, waving her hand vaguely to include me, Momo, and herself, "She'd probably collapse in shock!" Hana finished with a dramatic flourish, and I burst into laughter. The thought of their unorthodox relationship causing such a stir was absurd and somewhat amusing.

I let out a hearty chuckle, leaning back in my chair and musing, "Can you imagine? Her prim and proper daughter is living in sin in an intimate relationship with a man and a cat girl. She would probably have a heart attack."

Momo was practically howling with laughter, clutching her stomach as she wiped a tear from her eye. "Oh gosh, you should totally break it to her, Hana! Just think about her reaction. I mean, it would be totally worth it!"

Hana looked scandalized at the idea, holding a hand to her chest as if wounded. "I think I'd rather walk over hot coals, thank you very much." She grinned, rolling her eyes at Momo's suggestion. "No need to cause unnecessary cardiac problems for her."

I leaned forward, grinning mischievously at Hana. "Well, if you ever do decide to spill the beans, make sure I'm there. I wouldn't want to miss the show."

Momo's peals of laughter echoed in the room once more as we all fell into a comfortable, light-hearted silence. The gentle clink of chopsticks and the lingering aroma of ramen in the air created a soothing, homely atmosphere that felt just right. I had to admit, life with these two was never boring.

******

As we polished off the remnants of dinner, Momo casually chimed in, artfully slipping her question into the conversation. "Hana, you didn't forget about that new patch for 'League of Ancients,' did you? You know, the one everyone has been raving about? Apparently, it's not just an update - it's an overhaul. From what I've heard, it's a serious game-changer. Should make those infuriating balance issues vanish like smoke," she said, her expression perfectly composed, her poker face firmly in place.

"Wait, are you serious?" Hana's eyes sparkled with excited anticipation, her annoyance at the game's recent issues bubbling to the surface. "That's honestly awesome news. I was losing it the other night. I was so frustrated, I was about to quit the game for good."

"Yeah, I noticed," I chimed in, teasing her gently. "Our gaming sessions had taken a bit of a turn there. Your commentary on the in-game mic had become... quite vibrant. My ears are still ringing, like I just left a heavy metal concert."

Laughing off my comment, Hana stood, eager and determined. "Well, if that's the case, I better hustle and get this new patch downloaded. Maybe it'll temper my warpath a little. We should hop back on later tonight, show those noobs how we do things. Give them a taste of real gameplay."

As she stood and began her journey toward her room, she was blissfully unaware of the pleasant surprise that awaited her. Momo and I shared a secret glance, the corners of our mouths twitching with barely concealed amusement. A silent clap from Momo expressed her elation perfectly - she was practically vibrating with anticipation.

Then, it happened. The moment we'd been waiting for.

Hana's voice echoed throughout the apartment, her tone a perfect cocktail of shock, disbelief, and pure, unadulterated excitement. "Guys! Oh my god, guys!" She shouted, her voice carrying a note of wild exhilaration. "What the... what the fuck... I mean, seriously, what the actual fuck?"

Feigning confusion, but unable to wipe the smirk off my face, I called back, a hint of mischief twinkling in my eyes. "What's up, Hana? Something wrong?"

A sudden outburst echoed from the direction of Hana's room, jolting us back to reality. "Oh my gods, you two! This... This is a Titanforge! An actual, high-end, Titanforge gaming laptop!" Her voice was filled with disbelief, bubbling over with pure, unadulterated joy.

Struggling to suppress our grins, Momo and I exchanged a knowing glance. The cat was, indeed, out of the bag. The silence stretched, thick with anticipation, before Momo finally broke it, her gleeful giggles echoing in the room.

"Well, looks like our little surprise isn't a surprise anymore," she admitted, wiping a faux tear from her eye, her tone a playful mix of regret and satisfaction.

"Seems so," I added, my own smirk mirroring hers. The tension in the room dissipated, replaced by a warm, triumphant glow. Our secret was out, and it felt amazing.

Taking a moment to compose herself, Momo turned back in Hana's direction. "Yeah, Hana. It's all real. And it's all yours."

Her announcement hung in the air, filling the room with a tangible sense of joy. Now it was my turn to address Hana, my voice suddenly serious. "Hana, we care about you, a lot. You are an integral part of our lives, and we wanted to show our appreciation. And what better way to do that than with something we know you'd love? You deserve it, Hana. You deserve a beast of a machine that can match your incredible gaming skills. And besides, we just... we want to see you happy."

There was a moment of silence, followed by a soft sniffling sound. Hana emerged from her room, eyes brimming with unshed tears, her smile so wide it could light up the entire city. It was a sight to behold, one that tugged at our hearts.

"I... I don't even know what to say. You guys.. . this is... incredible. I'm overwhelmed. I... Thank you. Thank you so much!" Her words, choked out between sobs, filled the room, her happiness so profound it was nearly tangible.

The sight of Hana so touched, so genuinely moved, warmed my heart. The investment had been worth it - worth every single credit. "It's our pleasure, Hana," I replied, a soft smile playing on my lips. "And hey, cut the waterworks, alright? This is a celebration. Why don't you start that beast up and see what it can do?"

As Hana returned to her room, her steps light and full of newfound excitement, Momo and I shared a moment of contentment. Our surprise had been a grand success, and Hana's joy was the best reward we could have asked for.

CHAPTER 4

Half past eight found a weary Hana staggering into the Whisker Wonders office. She moved like a life-size puppet with broken strings, her feet barely leaving the carpet as she shambled toward her desk. It was plain as day she had been up all night, enthralled by her shiny new Titanforge gaming laptop.

"Rise and shine, Hana," I called out to her, an amused grin on my face. "You look like you've been through the ringer. I take it the new laptop was a hit?"

Her bleary eyes barely focused on me as she murmured something that sounded like a cross between a sigh and a groan. Then, she seemed to regain some semblance of her senses and turned a disgruntled glare my way. "Oh, you're a riot, Kazuki," she grumbled.

She shuffled past me, her aimless steps eventually leading her to the coffee machine. The sight that met her there, though, was enough to wake the dead. The coffee pot was tragically, horrifyingly empty. She stared at the void where her salvation was supposed to be, her despair echoing through the room.

"Is... is the coffee pot empty?" she stammered out, disbelief dripping from her words.

From her corner, Momo chimed in, an impish twinkle in her eyes. "Isn't the office coffee usually handled by the administrative assistant?" she teased, a smirk dancing on her lips.

I chuckled at Momo's clever jab, but Hana seemed less than amused. She shot a withering look at Momo, her eyes heavy with exhaustion. "Yes, Momo. I'm aware that making coffee is part of my job."

Momo snickered at Hana's response, her delight clear as day. "So, tell us, Hana. How late did you stay up gaming last night?"

Hana slouched against the counter, her shoulders sagging under the weight of her weariness. "I might have been up until 4," she confessed in a whisper.

Momo burst into laughter at that, her giggles filling the room. "The laptop's that good, huh?"

Worn out but still defiant, Hana squared her shoulders and met Momo's amused gaze. "It's too good, Momo. It might make me lose my job eventually."

Deciding to intervene, I cleared my throat and caught Momo's attention. "Hey, Momo, don't you think you're giving Hana enough of a hard time?"

Momo shrugged, her lips curving into a playful smile. "Just a bit of friendly teasing, Kazuki."

Next came Hana's trial by coffee. As I watched her grapple with the coffee-making process, I had to bite my lip to stop myself from laughing outright. At one point, she managed to rip the bag of coffee grounds open with so much gusto that it exploded, showering her and the counter with a brown, granulated mess. She stood there, blinking in shock, before launching an exasperated attempt to clean up her self-made disaster.

Through all this, her wearied mumblings provided the perfect soundtrack to her plight. "This is ridiculous," she grumbled, trying in vain to gather the spilled grounds. "I just wanted some coffee."

Finally, after what felt like an eternity, the coffee maker sprang to life, bubbling and hissing as it started brewing. Hana let out a sigh of relief, a small smile tugging at her lips.

"Finally," she murmured. "I've never worked this hard for a cup of coffee."

"Hana, the warrior of the coffee grounds," I joked, patting her on the back. She responded with a weary chuckle, her sense of humor still intact despite her exhaustion.

******

The steady murmur of the Whisker Wonders office, a symphony of typing keyboards, hushed conversations, and the occasional phone ring, took a backseat when Babs approached. Babs, our company's cat girl accountant, was as striking as she was distinctive. With her long, flowing, silver hair that glimmered like liquid mercury under the fluorescent office lights, she was always an eye-catching figure. Yet it was her piercing blue eyes, as captivating and deep as two azure oceans, that truly held a magnetism of their own. Every glance from those sapphire eyes, every spark of curiosity they held, drew people in.

"Kazuki, buried in work again?" Babs asked, her voice as smooth as a lullaby. Her feline agility was always impressive, and now she gracefully maneuvered her way onto the edge of my cluttered desk. Seeing her there, perched elegantly amongst my scattered reports and towering piles of paperwork, was akin to witnessing a beautiful painting come to life in a pile of chaos.

The sight of a pink, strawberry-glazed donut landing on my desk cut through my daze. It was placed neatly atop a napkin, the sweet scent wafting upwards and filling the air around us. I paused, pulling my eyes away from the mesmerizing sight of Babs and toward the unexpected treat. It was a welcome distraction from the relentless columns and cells of the Exceed spreadsheet that held my screen captive.

Taken aback, I blinked at the donut, then at Babs. "What's this?" I asked, more surprised than anything. The intensity of her gaze had a way of throwing me off balance. An undercurrent of jitteriness coursed through me as I felt the weight of her full attention on me.

With a soft, musical laugh that was reminiscent of a purr, Babs gestured toward the pastry. "Well, Kazuki, I happened to overhear you mentioning these strawberry donuts last week. I believe you said they were from that little bakery around the corner, right?"

I nodded, still slightly perplexed. "Yes, they make the best ones in town. But why...?"

A twinkle lit up her eyes, a soft curl playing at the corners of her lips. "Well, it seemed like a fitting way to say 'thank you'. You've been a great help with those tricky spreadsheets," she said, her voice filled with genuine gratitude. "Your knowledge of Exceed has significantly simplified my work, and I wanted to show my appreciation in some small way."

Her words made me blush, a warm heat creeping up my cheeks. Of course, I was always more than ready to lend a hand to my colleagues, but Babs' thankfulness felt... different. More personal, somehow. I noticed her lashes fluttering slightly, the way her tail swished with increased animation. I suspected that she harbored a crush on me, and it was making me uneasy.

Not because I wasn't flattered – it was more about how I was ill-equipped to handle such attention from another beautiful cat girl co-worker.

Feeling flustered, I scratched the back of my head. "Oh, it's no big deal, Babs. I was glad to assist. And, uh, thank you for the donut. It's... nice of you."

"Of course, Kazuki. It's the least I could do," she said, with a nod. Her eyes continued to sparkle, her tail swishing gently behind her.

Feeling a little overwhelmed, I offered her a shy smile before turning back to my computer screen, my fingers returning to the keyboard. The aroma of the strawberry donut lingered in the air, mixing with the scent of printed paper and coffee.

Sauntering over with her unmistakable air of poise, Momo joined the little gathering at my cubicle. She shot me a tight-lipped smile as her eyes, bright as two polished emeralds, quickly darted between Babs and myself. Those eyes, normally warm and inviting, were hinting at a little storm brewing behind them.

"Hey, Momo," I greeted, my voice betraying a tiny shred of nervousness. The mounting tension was a ticklish undercurrent, almost imperceptible but nonetheless present.

"Mornin', Kazuki," she responded, the corner of her mouth lifting in an off-kilter smile. She then shifted her attention to Babs, adopting a nonchalant air to mask her underlying irritation.

"Babs, I heard you've been having a bout with our beloved Wi-Fi, yeah?" Momo casually kicked off the conversation, the loaded question hanging in the air.

Babs laughed, her tail flicking behind her with amusement. "Oh, Momo, you won't believe it! The buffering was driving me nuts!"

Momo raised an eyebrow, her arms crossed over her chest as she leaned back on the edge of my cubicle. "Right? I mean, slow Wi-Fi is enough to send anyone over the edge!"

Babs nodded, her eyes twinkling with laughter. "Especially when you're knee-deep in a mess of spreadsheets!"

"Which is why we're on the same team, aren't we?" Momo shot back, her tone light but her gaze intense. "You keep the numbers in line, and I make sure the computers don't decide to take an unplanned vacation."

"And you, Kazuki," Babs interjected, shooting me a quick glance, "Keep everyone's spreadsheets in order, right?"

Caught off guard, I cleared my throat, my gaze drifting toward Momo, "I-I guess you could say that."

The air in the cubicle, now saturated with underlying currents of unspoken rivalry, was sliced by Momo's infectious laughter. "Well, you gotta admit, we're quite the team. Keeping the Whisker Wonders ship steady and sailing!"

Babs chimed in, a bright chuckle escaping her lips, "Absolutely! From accountancy to IT to the man behind all our spreadsheet magic. We're indispensable, each in our own unique ways!"

Through the laughter and jests, Momo's eyes never strayed far from me, still carrying that inscrutable spark of something I couldn't quite put my finger on. The conversation seemed to be veiled with multiple layers, a cocktail of humor, rivalry, and subtle tensions.

Suddenly I felt the vibration of my smartphone in my pants' pocket. I retrieved my phone and held it in front of my face for it to recognize me and unlock. Sure enough there was a brand new text from the green haired goddess herself.

Momo:

Hey Kazuki, what was the private conversation with Babs about? Why would she give you a strawberry donut, of all things? Since when does she play dessert delivery in the office?

Kazuki:

Hey Momo! Oh, it was nothing major. Babs was just saying thanks for all the help I've given her with her spreadsheet issues. The donut, well, that was a bit unexpected, but I guess it's her sweet way of expressing gratitude. And between you and me, I have to admit, the donut is pretty delicious!

Momo:

Interesting... Babs playing dessert delivery... that's new. And she seems to have picked your favorite flavor, what a coincidence! Did she mention why she suddenly felt the need to express her gratitude in this very specific and tasty manner? And you're enjoying it a bit too much, aren't you?

Kazuki:

Haha, Momo, you're overthinking it! She probably heard me talking about these strawberry donuts the other day and thought it'd make a nice thank you gift. And yes, I am enjoying it because, well, it's a donut! Who doesn't enjoy donuts?

Momo:

It's just odd. I've never seen her give anyone else a "thank you" donut before. It's as if she's trying to butter you up with pastries. Do you think there's a motive behind it?

Kazuki:

Hmm, are my eyes deceiving me or is there a hint of the green-eyed monster showing up in your texts, Momo?

Momo:

What? Me? Jealous? You're hilarious, Kazuki. Why would I be jealous? I mean, I'm sharing you with my best friend Hana, remember?

Kazuki:

LOL, Momo, when you put it like that... it does sound hilarious. Babs is just being friendly. I think you're reading too much into this.

Momo:

Maybe you're right, maybe I'm wrong. But it's just weird. Anyway, I won't let it bother me. Maybe I should also start distributing donuts in the office to compete with Babs.

Kazuki:

Haha, I see a fierce competition brewing. The Whisker Wonders Donut War is about to begin. Bring it on, Momo. Let's see who the real Donut Queen is.

Momo:

Oh, it's on, Kazuki. You better be prepared for the most intense donut competition of your life. The Donut Queen is ready for her reign!

Aiko snuck over and said with an icy voice. "I need you three to come to my office now."

CHAPTER 5

As the three of us were summoned, a sense of confusion and apprehension clouded our minds. The only indication we had was a cryptic message from Aiko, which only fueled our anxiety. The silent exchange of nervous glances between Momo, Hana, and myself as we ventured down the stern, carpeted hallway was testament to our collective unease.

Hana's murmurings barely made it to my ears, her voice just above a whisper. "Do you think we're in trouble?" Her eyes fluttered anxiously as she toyed with the sleeve of her shirt, deep in thought, trying to uncover any possible past incident that could have led to such an unexpected meeting.

Momo, always the one to lighten the mood, offered a casual shrug and a smug retort, "Who knows? Maybe Aiko has finally recognized my unparalleled I.T. skills and is about to promote me." We managed to stifle our chuckles, the banter offering a fleeting respite from our escalating worry. But as we neared Aiko's office, the humor faded and was replaced by an encroaching sense of formality.

Aiko's office, contrasting with our relaxed and friendly cubicles, held an air of intimidation. Aiko was poised and proper behind her grand, uncluttered desk. Her power suit, tailored to precision, seemed to mirror her personality, sharp and unyielding.

With a commanding tone that left no room for argument, Aiko gestured toward the chairs. "Please, have a seat." The three of us exchanged anxious looks before complying, the quiet room amplifying our mutual discomfort. I felt a surge of annoyance bubble up, my arms crossed over my chest as I matched Aiko's austere posture.

Without a hint of hesitation, Aiko cut straight to the chase, "Rumors have been circulating around the office, suggesting a romantic involvement among the three of you." The unexpected accusation threw us off balance. My eyes went wide with shock, irritation quickly giving way to a mixture of surprise and indignation.

"I beg your pardon?" I blurted out, the words echoing my disbelief. "Why should our personal lives be of any concern in our professional roles? This isn't an appropriate topic of discussion in a professional setting."

Momo and Hana were just as astounded by this unexpected interrogation. Momo's initial nonchalance had dissipated, replaced by a deep furrow of discontent. Hana's anxiety was evident, her eyes darting nervously between Momo and me.

The room fell silent once again, the tension a tangible entity as we waited for Aiko's response to my assertive rebuttal. The meeting, originally shrouded in mystery, had taken an unforeseen turn, leaving us shocked and slightly disturbed.

Unfazed by my retort, Aiko maintained her impassive gaze. She carefully opened a neatly arranged file on her desk, revealing an assortment of documents, the title 'Whisker Wonders – Office Policy' boldly embossed in black.

"Whisker Wonders is committed to transparency and maintaining a professional environment, and as such, we need to be aware of any relationships within the office," she articulated in her signature stern tone. "This isn't about invading your personal lives. It's about adherence to company policy, managing potential conflicts of interest, and promoting an unbiased work environment."

Her fingers methodically traced the lines of the document in front of her, "Section 4, Article 7 of our company policy clearly outlines that 'In the event of a romantic relationship between two or more employees, it must be disclosed to the Human Resources Department to mitigate any potential favoritism or perceived impropriety.'"

Her declaration sent waves of silence through the room. The stern formalism of the situation had transformed my initial annoyance into a burst of embarrassment. Casting a glance at Hana and Momo, I saw their faces mirroring my own befuddlement.

There we were, sitting in the silence of Aiko's office, with the cold reality of company policy reverberating in our ears. Our simple, carefree relationship had suddenly been spotlighted under the stringent lens of office regulations, catapulting us into a predicament we had never envisioned.

Aiko regarded us with a discerning eye, her gaze finally landing on me. She tilted her head slightly, an enigmatic smile pulling at her lips. "Kazuki, it appears you've managed to catch Babs' interest as well. It's fairly evident."

The revelation left me blinking in surprise, my brain working overtime to process the news. "Babs? Really?" I managed to stammer out. I had noticed the extra attention Babs had been giving me, sure, but I'd never expected it to evolve into something more. Especially not something that warranted a meeting with HR.

A giggle erupted from Momo's direction, and I glanced over to see both her and Hana exchanging smug grins. Their amusement at my flabbergasted expression was hardly concealed. "Kaz, you're so dense sometimes," Momo said, her voice lilting with mirth. She folded her arms across her chest, trying to appear stern but the corners of her lips twitched upward, betraying her facade.

"Yeah," Hana chimed in, adding a playful nudge. "You're as oblivious as a mole in sunglasses. Seriously, it's like, totally obvious."

I rubbed the back of my neck, feeling the flush of embarrassment rising up my cheeks. I was about to retort when Aiko's stern voice cut through the levity.

"The situation, as you can see," Aiko said, her gaze sweeping over the three of us, "is complicated. With your involvement with not one, not two, but three women in this office, Kazuki, there are bound to be issues."

She folded her hands on the desk, creating a barrier of sorts. It was as if she was preparing herself for a battle. "Imagine, for instance, if things go sour. The fallout, the emotional upheaval... it would inevitably spill over into the workplace. It's a ticking time bomb of drama waiting to happen. And frankly, that's not a situation we want to be dealing with."

The weight of her words made the room feel a little colder, a little sterner. I felt my throat tighten. I had known that things could get complex but hearing it laid out so bluntly was a bit unsettling.

"This," Aiko continued, leaning back in her chair, "is precisely the reason I had reservations when Sakura decided to bring you on board. She insisted, of course, and your performance thus far has been commendable. However, potential interpersonal issues were a concern from the beginning."

A sinking feeling filled my stomach. The fact that my employment had caused such a behind-the-scenes debate was a shock. I had been blissfully unaware, simply focusing on doing the best job I could. All I could do was hope that my performance so far had validated Sakura's decision to hire me.

Aiko's voice pulled me back from my thoughts. "I should mention that Sakura has been made aware of the recent developments. Whether she decides to discuss it with you directly is her call."

I was left reeling in the aftermath of the conversation. The whole thing felt like a soap opera unfolding right in the HR department of Whisker Wonders. I found it almost funny how my love life had somehow transformed into a modern sitcom plotline, creating waves in the serene sea that was usually the office environment. Who knew love could be this complicated?

******

When we managed to extricate ourselves from the bureaucratic nerve center that was Aiko's office, we found ourselves ambling back toward my cubicle, a newfound closeness radiating from the three of us. The air was practically saturated with the leftovers of that strange tension, transforming the usual busy office atmosphere into a surreal workplace drama backdrop.

"I mean, seriously you guys," Momo kicked off the post-meeting analysis as we reached my cubicle, the disbelief still dancing in her eyes. Her voice was a hushed whisper, a clandestine soundtrack to our whispered conference. "Did we just step out of an episode of 'Office Romantics: The Unexpected Triad' or what?"

Her question elicited soft laughter from Hana and me, a shared humor that rippled through our little group and echoed around my cubicle. "I know, right?" Hana chimed in, the chuckle in her voice a gentle ebb and flow amidst our covert conversation. "It was just so...unexpected. I mean, who anticipates a dramatic intervention at work, right?"

As the three of us huddled around my desk, close enough for our whispers to intermingle without catching unwanted attention, we dissected the whole interaction, laughter acting as our main defense mechanism. But behind their laughter, I could see the lingering uncertainty, the questions unasked.

"But guys," Hana's voice was barely audible as she voiced the concern that had started to creep into the edges of our light-hearted chatter. "Do you think...do you think this changes anything for us?"

The question seemed to halt everything around us, even the fluorescent office lights seemed to dim, awaiting my answer. I shook my head, my words cutting through the brief silence, "No, absolutely not. We're way stronger than a few office rumors or Aiko's misguided concerns. Remember, we care deeply for each other. This isn't going to change... from my end at least.."

The relief that swept across Momo's face was almost tangible. "Right," she echoed, her smile returning full force. Her eyes twinkling, she winked, "And

besides, who can resist our epic, out-of-this-world..."
she paused for dramatic effect, a faint blush creeping
up her cheeks, "gaming sessions?"

Hana caught on to Momo's playful innuendo,
erupting into a fit of giggles, a cathartic release that
melted away the residual tension. "Oh yeah," she managed to sputter between bouts of laughter. "Our gaming 'threesomes' are simply irresistible, Kaz. Admit it."

Their infectious laughter spilled over, enveloping
me in a bubble of hilarity. As we continued laughing
at the ludicrous situation, my gaze caught Babs across
the office. She was watching us, her eyebrows furrowed in confusion, an undercurrent of what seemed
like lust in her gaze. It was a scene right out of a sitcom,
and that absurdity just made our shared moment funnier.

Navigating an office romance was one thing, but
add in a jealous coworker and HR intervention, and
you have the makings of a comedic masterpiece. However, if this was my new reality, these two remarkable
women were my friends, my lovers, and my gaming
buddies. No HR policy could dictate the terms of our
relationship.

With that defiant thought in my mind, we dissolved into another round of silent laughter, oblivious to the curious glances directed our way. We had just survived our first, and hopefully last, HR intervention, and that was certainly an achievement worth celebrating.

A sharp, staccato symphony of high heels reverberated through the office, heralding the approach of our formidable HR manager, Aiko. Her footsteps echoed like the steady drumroll before a nerve-wracking performance, only, this wasn't a performance, but reality. She stepped from the secluded fortress of her office, shooting icy, pointed glares our way, which felt like they could freeze us on the spot. Her stern 'hmph' cleared the air but bore the weight of a much louder message - 'Back to work, now.'

"Oh, damn, guys! We've rattled the HR lady!" Momo's whispered voice, mimicking Aiko's frosty tone with such accuracy it was almost scary, broke the tense silence. Her words rolled with a touch of mischief, her eyes twinkling in amusement at our clandestine huddle.

Hana's laughter rang out, vibrant and infectious, a melody amidst the silent, ominous atmosphere.

"Momo, you're just nailing it! Imagine Aiko hearing this one day, it would be priceless!" she exclaimed, barely containing her giggles.

Under the weight of Aiko's persistent, frosty stare, I responded, trying to suppress my own amusement, "Guys, I think it's time to wave the white flag. Let's reconvene at our safe zone - the lunch table later."

"But, Kazuki," Hana chimed in, a mischievous glint in her eyes, "we could keep this up over text, right? Maybe even throw in some...spicier content?" She waggled her eyebrows suggestively, a playfully naughty jest adding a dash of thrill to our scandalous conversation.

Just then, Aiko cleared her throat once more, her resounding 'hmph' ringing louder than before. That was it – game over. The fun and games dissipated as Hana and Momo darted back to their desks like soldiers retreating. The three of us shared a knowing grin before returning to our duties. As we scattered back to our work, our lighthearted moment of rebellion was just a memory, but lunchtime was always just a few hours away.

The atmosphere of the office was tensely silent, the heavy air almost seeming to congeal around me. Suddenly, my phone blasted its notification alert with startling fervor, punctuating the quiet with a jarring vibration against the wooden surface of my desk. In my post-meeting stress, I had completely forgotten to put my smartphone on vibrate.

As I glanced down at the buzzing menace, a familiar pang of excitement and apprehension shot through me. The screen lit up to reveal a group text notification from Hana and Momo. I found my lips curving upwards into a reluctant smile, my fatigue momentarily forgotten as I prepared myself for the wild ride that was undoubtedly about to unfold in the form of our group chat shenanigans.

My fingertips made contact with the screen, deftly unlocking the device and navigating to the messages app. As I clicked on the conversation thread, I was met with a barrage of colorful, chaotic text bubbles. I couldn't stifle a chuckle at the sight; the infectious energy that Hana and Momo brought to even the most mundane interactions was one of the many reasons I enjoyed their company so much.

The conversation was already lively, each message filled with their signature brand of humor and quirky emoticons.

Hana: *Phew, we barely escaped with our lives there, comrades! Are you sweating bullets too, Kazuki?*

Momo: *Talk about walking into enemy territory, Kazuki. You owe us big time. We just took some serious battle scars in there, you know.*

I quickly typed a response, my fingers dancing across the screen as I tried to match their playful banter.

Kazuki: *Her eyes could freeze lava, seriously, did you guys see that? It was like she was trying to turn us into stone!*

Hana: *Stone or not, our fiery spirits remain unquenchable haha. And don't forget the sizzling hot texts we'll bombard you with. Prepare yourself, Kazuki.*

Momo: *I bet he's blushing already. We can see you from here, you know! Watch out, Kazuki, the walls have eyes!

I shot back, injecting a hint of threat into my words to balance the humor.

Kazuki: *Very funny, Momo. Keep that up and see if you get any of the ramen I'm making tonight. Don't think I won't hold it hostage.

Hana: *Wait, did someone say ramen? My allegiance is easily bought, Kazuki. Now, about those spicy texts...

Momo: *Can you imagine if Aiko saw these? She might just burst into flames.

I found myself laughing under my breath at our ridiculous exchange, my initial stress and fear fading away as I let myself be swept up in our humorous banter. It was moments like these that reminded me of why I wouldn't trade my complicated relationship with Hana and Momo for anything in the world. Even if it meant occasionally having to endure Aiko's icy stare.

Kazuki: *Guys, seriously though, have you noticed how silent Sakura has been? And that perpetual mysterious look... it's like she's trying to solve the riddles of the universe.

Hana: *Oh, definitely. She's got that "I'm con-templating the mysteries of life, the universe, and everything" stare down to an art form.

Momo: *Yes, when she's not silently critiquing us from behind those striking blue eyes of hers. It's like she's got her very own drama-seeking radar.

Kazuki: *I swear, I sometimes feel like she's try-ing to burn holes through me with her gaze alone. If looks could be weaponized...

Hana: *I bet she's just trying to crack your ramen recipe, Kazuki. Got any secret ingredients we should be worried about?

Kazuki: *Oh, the secret ingredient? It's pure hard work and the unique stress of managing you two.

Momo: *So, that's the 'extra spice' huh? Can we add 'Sakura's laser-focused judgement stare' to the list too? Might make for an interesting taste.

Kazuki: *If her stares were lethal, we would all have been turned into mush by now, let's be honest.

Hana: *In the unlikely event that I do get turned into mush, Kazuki, promise me you'll make me into shrimp mush.

Kazuki: *I... I don't even know how to respond to that. If any of you turned into shrimp mush, I'd... well, let's just hope it doesn't come to that.

Momo: *But imagine it, Kazuki, a world without us to annoy you, to make ramen for, to send flirty texts. A silent, desolate, ramen-less world. Now that's a horrifying thought.

Kazuki: *Okay, that's just... Let's stick to the topic at hand. Any idea what's going on in Sakura's head? Is she going to have a meeting with us, you think?

Hana: *Who knows, Kazuki? Maybe she's designing a new spreadsheet system or devising a way to add more spice to your ramen. The possibilities are endless with Sakura.

Kazuki: *As much as I'd love to imagine her as the ramen-obsessed villain in this scenario, I'm more worried about what she might do in reality.

Momo: *Well, you know what they say, 'Keep your friends close and your HR Managers and CEOs closer.' Seems particularly relevant in this case.

Hana: *Exactly! And remember, if we get turned into shrimp mush, at least we know we'll be delicious.

Kazuki: *God, what are we even talking about? None of this makes sense. How did we get onto the mush shit. You two... are impossible. Let's just hope for the best.

Momo. *What the hell are we talking about?*

***Kazuki:** *Alright, ladies, I think it's time to hit pause on our virtual rendezvous. As much as I enjoy our little distraction, I'm worried Aiko might start noticing our flagrant disregard of her beloved rules.*

Hana: *Oh come on, Kazuki! You're such a party pooper. Can't we keep the fun going for just a bit longer? You must admit, this is far more exciting than staring at spreadsheets all day...

Momo: *I second that, Kazuki. Don't be such a stick in the mud! What's the harm in a few extra minutes away from our keyboards? It's not like we're throwing a full-on party in the middle of the office... or are we?

Kazuki: *As enticing as a midday office party sounds, I don't think Aiko would be too amused. We have been pushing our luck quite a bit.

Hana: *But Kazuki, think about it. What if we establish a system? Like, for every hour of intense work, we get a five-minute fun break. Sounds fair, right?

Kazuki: *Hana, as much as I appreciate your diplomatic approach, I'm not sure our productivity—or Aiko—would survive your proposal.*

Momo: *Oh, Kazuki, always the voice of reason! But what else can we expect from our dedicated worker bee? Hana, it looks like we've been outvoted. Back to the grindstone, I guess.*

Hana: *I suppose you're right, Momo. Fine, we surrender! But Kazuki, just so you know, we reserve the right to make your professional life... let's say, intriguing.*

Kazuki: *Oh, I have no doubt about that. But for now, let's put our noses to the grindstone, shall we? At least until our stomachs start grumbling for lunch.*

Hana: *Alright, we have a deal. But don't forget, you owe us for this. Big time.*

Momo: *Absolutely, Kazuki! Remember, we'll be expecting a handsome reward for our compliance.*

Kazuki: *Well, I suppose that's only fair. But for now, let's buckle down and show Aiko we can be just as dedicated to our tasks as we are to our... extracurricular activities.*

Hana: *Agreed. But remember, Kazuki, we will not let you forget this. You will make it up to us. Eventually.*

Momo: *Definitely, Hana. For now, back to the grind. But Kazuki, know this, we will hold you to your promise. This is not the end of our little adventure.

Kazuki: *Trust me, ladies, I wouldn't have it any other way. Now, let's bury ourselves in work before Aiko catches us for the umpteenth time.*

CHAPTER 6

The pungent aroma of sweat permeated the air as I stepped onto the worn mats of the dojo. I bowed respectfully to the lone figure awaiting me - my friend and fellow martial artist, Chozen. Though we followed different disciplines - his rooted in traditional Karate, mine honed through the subtleties of Wing Chun Kung Fu - we often met here to test our skills in combat.

Chozen returned my bow, his expression stoic, giving no indication of the coming duel. "It's been a awhile, Kazuki," he remarked. His voice was gravelly yet edged with precision.

I nodded. "Yes, nearly a week since we last sparred. How have you been, Chozen?"

"Well enough," he replied plainly. Chozen had never been one for idle chatter. Without another word, he began to stretch and warm up, executing crisp, powerful karate techniques - each punch, kick and block perfectly precise.

I followed his lead, flowing through my own warm-up routine focused on the nuances of Wing Chun - relaxed limbs, agile footwork and rapid-fire chain punches. We prepared in silence, the only sounds being that of controlled breathing and the squeak of the mats under our motions.

After several minutes, Chozen ceased his movements and faced me, his gaze penetrating. "Let us see how much you've practiced since our last bout, Kazuki," he challenged, dropping into a low karate stance.

I nodded, shifting into my own Wing Chun stance - knees bent, elbows in, hands loose and ready. "I look forward to an interesting match, my friend."

Chozen suddenly exploded forward with startling speed, aiming a powerful reverse punch straight for my torso. Prepared for his aggression, I reacted immediately, executing a swift Bong Sau block to redirect the force of the blow off to my right side. Before he could pull back I countered, delivering a rapid chain punch toward his chest. He managed to divert the first two strikes but the third landed cleanly.

"Good, you've been practicing," Chozen remarked, seemingly unfazed by the hit. He pressed forward again, unleashing a barrage of quick, successive punches. I met them head on, using my elbows and forearms to block and deflect the worst of the blows. Several still landed, leaving faint aches. I bit back any reaction - I wouldn't show weakness here.

Seeing his punches having only limited effect, Chozen switched tactics, launching into a spinning back kick. I quickly shifted my body, avoiding the strike by mere inches. In the same fluid motion I aimed an upward palm strike at his shoulder as he finished the kick. The blow clearly caught him off guard.

"Your reflexes have improved as well," Chozen noted. He gave no indication if my strike had caused him pain. I realized I would get no such reaction. I pressed my momentary advantage, using swift footwork to angle around him while unleashing more chain punches. He blocked them admirably but I still managed to land a kidney shot that elicited a faint grunt from him.

Before he could counterattack I swept his front leg out from under him in one smooth motion. He hit the mats hard but recovered swiftly, springing back up to face me. The faintest hint of a smile pulled at his lips. "You've learned some new tricks it seems."

I returned the smile briefly. "As have you, I suspect." No sooner had I finished speaking than he launched into a spinning hook kick. I reacted just in time, intercepting the strike with a Tan Sau block. As I completed the block I aimed my own kick at his midsection which he only narrowly avoided.

Back and forth we exchanged blows at a mounting tempo - each testing the other's defenses, seeking openings to exploit. I managed to break through his guard with a deceptive straight punch, following up swiftly with a barrage of body blows. He took the hits with only a faint grimace.

Just when I thought I had gained the upper hand, he countered with blistering speed, raining down an onslaught of knife-hand strikes. I was hard pressed to block them all, feeling several slice painfully into my shoulders before I could break away. Now it was my turn to hide any reaction.

We paused our duel for a moment, breathing heavily as we circled each other. Our eyes remained locked, silently probing for any weakness. In the same instant we both struck, meeting a collision of fists and feet. He landed a hard side kick to my thigh as my punch glanced off his shoulder. We broke apart from the exchange evenly matched.

"You continue to impress, my friend," Chozen conceded, rolling his injured shoulder gingerly. "But as you can see, my Karate skills have only sharpened since our last encounter."

I nodded, discreetly rubbing my thigh where a bruise would undoubtedly form. "As have my Wing Chun techniques. But the night is still young," I said, dropping back into a ready stance.

Chozen's eyes glinted with enthusiasm and he beckoned me forward. "Then let us continue this contest."

At his invitation I exploded forward, raining down a blur of rapid punches coupled with deceptive footwork to keep him off balance. He blocked and evaded well, but my combinations were too swift and precise. I landed a one-inch punch squarely to his solar plexus, momentarily knocking the wind from him. I followed it up swiftly with a sweeping kick to take his legs out once again.

He slammed into the mats hard, my leg sweep having affected his balance significantly. But his gaze remained fiery and determined. As he started to rise I moved in, ready to decisively end the bout. With lightning reflexes I boxed his ears simultaneously with both palms, the Twin Palms technique creating an intense vertigo effect. Before he could recover from the disorienting blow I wrapped up the match, stopping a straight punch just short of his face.

I stepped back and extended a hand to help Chozen up. He grasped it firmly, rising to his feet with as much dignity as he could muster. For a long moment we simply looked at each other, no words necessary. We were both warriors and understood that in combat, there were always victories and defeats.

Finally I broke the silence. "You fought exception-ally well, my friend. It was an honor to test my skills against you." I finished with a respectful bow.

Chozen returned the bow. "The honor was mine," he replied solemnly. "You bested me fair and square. Your Wing Chun has reached an impressive level of skill." He rolled his shoulder once more and gave me the faintest of smiles. "Same time next week?"

I returned the smile sincerely as I gathered my be-longings. Our sparring sessions were always learning experiences, regardless of the outcome. "I look for-ward to it." I gave him one last bow before exiting the dojo, the lingering thrill of victory keeping my steps light. Though different in style, our shared devotion to martial arts brought us together as worthy adver-saries and true friends.

CHAPTER 7

S tepping through the glossy front doors, I was enveloped by the contagious energy of Truck-Kun & More anime shop. Upbeat Japanese pop blasted loudly through overhead speakers, competing with the enthusiastic murmur of diverse patrons filling the aisles.

My eyes darted around trying to absorb it all - display cases of intricate figurines, shelves bursting with vibrant manga, racks overloaded with whimsical accessories. Teens laughed nearby over outrageous meme keychains while a pair of dwarves debated collectible vinyl figures.

In the clothing section, a stylish drow tried on a leather jacket with fiery phoenix art as his friend looked on approvingly. Nearby, a goblin girl happily modeled an oversized sweater featuring a cute chibi yeti design.

A dragonborn woman scrutinized enamel pins of characters from series like "Card Crusade" and "Mecha Arena." The air was saturated with lively discussion and shared excitement. As I admired a sprawling mural of anime heroes and villains locked in epic combat, a cheerful voice called out.

"Welcome to Truck-Kun & More! Let me know if you need help finding anything." I turned to see a grinning lizardman clerk approaching, his name tag identifying him as Razzik. He flashed me a wide, toothy smile, his yellow slit-pupiled eyes filled with friendliness.

"Thank you," I replied, "I'm looking to find some anime character statues for gifts."

Razzik's eyes lit up, pupils dilating with interest. "We can certainly help you with that sir! Our newest Venus & Valkyrie line just arrived and the detailing is remarkable." He beckoned for me to follow him through the organized chaos of merchandise.

As we walked, he asked, "So what series are they fans of? That'll help me suggest the perfect statues!"

I described, "Well Hana loves fantasy adventures like 'Elysian Chronicles.' And Momo is obsessed with sci-fi mecha shows like 'Tech Fighters Zero.'"

Razzik nodded along eagerly, tail swishing behind him. "We have a massive collection from those series. I'll take you to our statue section right away!" As we maneuvered through the maze of aisles, he queried, "Have you seen those shows yourself?"

I shook my head ruefully. "I haven't yet, though I've heard great things. I always seem to get distracted by other anime."

Razzik clicked his tongue disapprovingly. "Well, nothing beats my personal favorite, 'Ramen Samurai!' It has drama, incredible fight scenes, and the most lovable characters ever."

I raised my eyebrows, intrigued by his passion. "Oh yeah? What makes it so special?"

His pupils dilated again, enthusiasm brimming over. "What doesn't it have? The story sucks you in right away and never lets up. And the ramen scenes will make you drool nonstop. You have to add it to your watch list!"

I chuckled, promising I would check it out based on his compelling endorsement. We soon arrived at the elaborate character statues. My eyes darted over the intricate recreations of heroes, villains, monsters and more.

After much deliberation, I selected a beautifully crafted sorceress from 'Elysian Chronicles' for Hana and a fierce mecha pilot model from 'Tech Fighters Zero' for Momo.

Razzik applauded my choices as he rang them up. "You clearly know how to pick pieces they'll appreciate!" he praised. "Feel free to come by anytime for more recommendations. It was great meeting a fellow anime fan!"

I thanked him sincerely for his enthusiastic help before turning to leave, bag in hand. Stepping outside, the sun's warmth welcomed me as I considered the meaning behind my purchases. The statues reflected the fantasy worlds Hana, Momo and I often escaped into. Smiling, I strolled off, eager to see Hana and

Momo's reactions to these gifts. I hoped that they would like them.

******

Bag in hand containing my treasured gifts, I stepped out into the streets with a satisfied smile. The cool breeze on my face was as welcoming as the shop's interior had been. With a contented sigh, I turned to begin the eight-block stroll to Hana and Momo's apartment.

I soon fell into a comfortable pace, breathing in the city air, fragrant with aromas from street food vendors mixed with engine exhaust. The buildings rose around me, an endless concrete and glass forest interspersed with small shops displaying their colorful wares.

I passed a snow cone vendor with a line of parents and children. The owner called out lively greetings to every customer. Next was a boutique proudly show-casing frilly maid outfits and cat-ear headbands in its window. I was lucky to have authentic cat girls. I do wonder how hot they would look in those maid out-fits.

Further down I spotted a steak restaurant just opening for the supper rush, while across the street an occult store displayed ominous crystal balls and bundles of sage. It looked like something you would see in New Orleans. This neighborhood always had such fascinating variety.

About halfway into my walk, I noticed a drop dead gorgeous kitsune girl approaching from the opposite direction. She appeared to be in her early 20s, with piercing amber eyes and lustrous auburn hair that tumbled over her shoulders in gentle waves. Her most eye-catching features were the five bushy tails swishing playfully behind her. Kitsune girls were always hot as hell in the anime and manga from Earth. They were even hotter in the flesh.

As she drew closer, her face broke into a radiant smile. "Well aren't you quite the handsome man!" she called out. I blinked in surprise, unsure how to respond. She carried an air of confidence, walking with a noticeable sway in her step. I looked behind me to see if she was talking to someone else.

She paused right in front of me, practically forcing me to stop. "Yes I was talking to you. What's got you all flustered?" she teased, noticing my awkwardness.

"Oh, uh, nothing," I stammered. "Just didn't expect to be called handsome out of the blue. That's not something that happens very often... we'll it doesn't happen at all."

She laughed, a melodic sound at odds with her boldness. "Just telling it like it is," she said with a flirtatious wink. "But what's got you looking so satisfied? I saw a big smile on your face from a distance. Hot date tonight?"

"What? Oh, no, nothing like that," I insisted, feeling my cheeks heat up. "I was just doing some shopping for gifts." I held up the bag sheepishly.

"Gifts, huh? Now I'm really curious who the lucky lady is!" Her eyes positively sparkled with mischief as she edged closer. Up close, she smelled faintly of cherry blossoms.

"They're for my girlfriends actually," I explained, hoping that detail would discourage her attention. But instead, her eyes lit up even more.

"Oooh, girlfriends?" she asked eagerly. "As in plural? Aren't you quite the heartbreaker!" She playfully nudged my arm. "Do tell, what's the story there?"

I rubbed my neck, unsure why I was revealing personal details to this overly friendly stranger. "Well, it's a bit unconventional I guess. I'm dating two cat girls who are actually best friends. We just kind of clicked."

The kitsune girl looked thoughtful, tapping a claw-tipped finger on her chin. "You don't say... that's an intriguing setup! And they're alright with sharing you?" She sidled even closer, forcing me to take a half step back.

"Yeah, we make it work," I said simply, hoping she would lose interest. No such luck though. She continued eyeing me up and down appreciatively.

"Well now, aren't you a lucky one! Such a handsome guy with not just one, but two lovely ladies!" She leaned in close, her words almost a purr. "Maybe you'd consider adding a third to really spice things up?"

My eyes widened at her audacity. "That's, uh, quite a bold offer," I stammered. "But I really should get going. My girlfriends are expecting me." I tried to skirt around her but she blocked my path, unwilling to end our encounter.

Her tails swished behind her as she pressed on. "Oh come now, don't run off just yet. Why don't we exchange numbers? We could meet up, have some fun. .." She trailed a clawed fingertip slowly down my arm.

I gently pulled my arm away, trying to let her down easy. "That's flattering, really. But like I said, I'm in a relationship. Two relationships, actually. I need to get going."

She pouted dramatically but finally relented. "You're no fun! But if you change your mind..." She held out a business card with a wink.

I shook my head politely. "I appreciate the offer, but my girlfriends are all I can handle." We exchanged brief, awkward goodbyes before I hurried on.

I breathed a sigh of relief to end the encounter with the overly eager kitsune. The whole interaction had caught me totally off guard. But soon the sights and sounds of the neighborhood pulled me back in. A few blocks later I arrived at Hana and Momo's apartment, gifts in tow and an amusing story to tell.

******

Gripping the bag containing my treasured gifts, I approached the familiar apartment door, eager to see what reactions my surprises would elicit. I fished out my key, stepping inside to the welcoming ambiance I knew so well.

"Hana, Momo, I'm back!" I called out. Moments later, the two cat girls emerged from the living room, their faces lighting up at my arrival.

"Hey you!" Hana greeted me warmly before her gaze fell to the bag in my hand, her eyes widening with interest. "Ooh, whatcha got there?"

"Yeah, what'd you bring us, Kazuki?" Momo chimed in eagerly, trying to sneak a peek into the bag's contents.

I laughed and playfully held it just out of reach. "Wouldn't you two like to know?" I teased. "Who says this is even for you? Maybe I've taken up a new hobby."

Hana's eyes went wide, her lower lip pushing out in an exaggerated pout. "What? Kazuki, how could you be so mean?" She implored, dramatically placing the back of her hand on her forehead. "You can't just arrive with a mysterious bag and not expect us curious kitties to be absolutely dying to know what's inside!"

"Yeah, our inquiring minds need to know!" Momo insisted, matching Hana's theatrical tone. She leaned in close, looking up at me with their beautiful eyes, hands clasped together pleadingly. "Come on, just a teensy hint? Give us something, please?"

I chuckled at their transparent eagerness, enjoying dragging out their anticipation just a bit longer. "Alright, alright, one very small hint," I relented, watching their faces light up. "This is something we all share a strong interest in, something we enjoy doing together quite often."

"A shared interest?" Hana tapped her chin thoughtfully before gasping. "I bet it's a new multiplayer game for us to try out!"

"Ohh yes, it must be!" Momo's eyes shone eagerly. "Kazuki knows we love gaming together. He wouldn't be able to resist getting us something new to play co-op or competitively!" She high-fived Hana in excitement before they both turned expectantly to me.

I simply shrugged, trying not to crack. "Not even close, ladies. You're way off the mark with that guess."

Their crestfallen, confused reactions made me have to stifle a laugh. "But don't look so down," I encouraged. "You'll find out soon enough what's in the bag."

Hana shook her head in dramatic dismay. "The agony of suspense! This is torturous, Kazuki!" She clasped her hands together pleadingly, eyes wide and imploring. "Can't you take pity and show us already, pretty please?"

Momo quickly mirrored her posture, hands together in a begging gesture. "We're positively dying from curiosity here!" she declared. "Have mercy and reveal your secrets, I beg you!" Their silly theatrics were admittedly quite cute and endearing.

I pretended to consider for a moment before chuckling. "Alright, I suppose you two have suffered enough. I'll finally put you out of your misery." I reached into the bag, watching their eyes widen as I slowly drew out the two anime statues.

"Oh my gosh, these are amazing!" Hana gasped, reverently taking the intricately detailed sorceress figurine I'd picked out for her. She turned it over gently in her hands, utterly transfixed. "Just look at all these tiny details in her robes, her staff, even her jewelry! It's incredible!"

Meanwhile, Momo was utterly fixated on the mecha pilot model, intended specially for her. "This is too perfect!" she exclaimed, carefully but eagerly examining it from multiple angles. "The detailing is so precise, even on the back of the mech! I can see all the individual missile hatches and thrusters!"

I smiled happily, warmed by their obvious joy and excitement over the gifts. "I saw these statues and immediately thought you two would love them. I'm really glad you do."

Hana carefully set down her sorceress figurine and suddenly threw her arms around me in an enthusiastic hug. "Like them? We absolutely LOVE them!" she declared intensely. She squeezed me tight, practically bouncing up and down in glee. "You're the most thoughtful, wonderful, amazing boyfriend ever!"

As Hana finally released me from her ecstatic embrace, Momo stepped forward and wrapped me in a hug of her own. "These gifts are so incredibly thoughtful and perfect," she said sincerely, leaning up on her tiptoes to give me an affectionate peck on the cheek. "You just get us and what we love so well. That means everything."

"Well, I do try my best," I chuckled, truly touched by their heartfelt reactions. Seeing how much the anime statues clearly resonated with them made all the time and effort deciding on just the right gifts completely worthwhile.

Hana picked up her sorceress figurine again, tenderly tracing her fingertips over the delicate details as if worried she'd somehow damage the intricate craftsmanship. "It really is perfect, Kazuki. Now I'll get to see her casting spells and working magic every single day on my desk!"

"And I can imagine my mecha pilot fighting epic space battles right there next to my keyboard!" Momo added eagerly, admiration shining in her eyes as she continued examining the precise detailing on her statue. "It's like having a piece of the shows we love so much right there with us always."

I smiled happily, thrilled that the statues carried even deeper meaning about our shared interests and time spent together. Just as I'd hoped, they appreciated how the fantasy worlds we so often escaped to now had a physical presence in our reality to enjoy.

Momo reverently set down her mecha pilot figure before turning and pulling me into another grateful hug. "Seriously Kazuki, this means so much to us," she said warmly, nestling against me. "The actual gifts are amazing, but it's the thought and care that went into choosing them that we truly love."

"Absolutely!" Hana readily agreed, setting her sorceress down and joining our hug so I was enveloped in both their embraces. "You just get us so incredibly well. Knowing you put that much thought into picking the perfect gifts means everything."

I gladly returned their affectionate hugs, feeling a profound sense of contentment. I was sincerely touched by their heartfelt responses. "You two are worth all the thought put into those gifts and infinitely more," I replied genuinely.

As we finally stepped apart, the sheer joy sparkling in both their eyes was the only reward I needed. Though the fantasy worlds the statues represented were imaginary, the happiness they'd clearly brought Hana and Momo was very real. And there were few greater joys than being able to bring such delight to the two women I cared so deeply for.

Momo turned and carefully picked up her mecha pilot statue again, admiring it with a warm smile. "I just love all the little details so much," she remarked, pointing out the intricately etched control panels and thruster ports that an untrained eye could easily miss. "It really shows how much care the sculptor put into bringing this character to life."

"I know, it's incredible work!" Hana agreed, joining Momo in closely examining the statues. "Like just look at how precise the folds and runes are on my sorceress's robes. You can tell how dedicated the artist was to capturing everything that makes her special."

Her words made me think of my own dedication to capturing what made Hana and Momo special when picking out their gifts. I suddenly asked, "So which details on the statues really stood out to you both? What resonated most?"

Hana's face scrunched up adorably in thought. "Hmm, well for me it's the little designs etched into the sorceress's staff," she decided after a moment.

"They're so intricate despite being so tiny, just like the spellcasting details in the show. It's gorgeous!"

Momo nodded enthusiastically. "And for me, it's all the tiny warning labels and control buttons in the mech cockpit," she added. "It reminds me of how the show always highlighted the pilot's connection to his machine. I just love that!"

Their perspectives made me smile. "I'm really glad you noticed those little elements," I told them sincerely. "When I saw them in the shop, they stood out just like that for me too. So I hoped they'd excite you both the same way."

Hana's eyes shone, touched by my words. "Aww, I love that even more!" she exclaimed, pulling me into yet another delighted hug. "It's like you picked out special details just for each of us. Seriously, this gift couldn't be any more perfect!"

As Hana finally released me, Momo gave me a quick grateful peck on the lips, her eyes full of warmth. "She's absolutely right, that makes it even more special and meaningful," Momo agreed happily. "Only you would think of choosing statues so specifically catered to our unique interests, Kazuki."

"Well, I can't take all the credit," I chuckled. "You two are my inspiration, after all." I drew them both in close again, so happy I could share this moment of joy with them.

Hana giggled, snuggling against me contentedly. "You're too sweet, Kazuki! But the credit is definitely yours." She reached out and put her hand atop Momo's, both their hands resting on my chest over my heart. "This came from you and your thoughtfulness," Hana said with certainty.

Momo nodded her agreement, squeezing my hand affectionately. "Completely!" she declared. "So just take our gratitude, because you've more than earned it today." Her words filled me with a deep sense of fulfillment.

As I stood there enveloped in their warmth, I felt profoundly blessed to have not just one, but two incredible women in my life who I cared for so deeply, and who cared for me just the same. The fantasy worlds that brought us joy were imaginary, but this - this connection we shared - was my reality. And I wouldn't trade it for anything.

As they gingerly held their new treasures, Momo and Hana's eyes locked in a mutual understanding. Their expressions were subtle, their silent communication almost invisible to the untrained eye, but I had spent enough time with them to recognize that particular exchange. It was a look that spelled a sudden change in atmosphere, a shift from innocent delight to something more heated.

Their irises sparkled, reflecting the soft ambient lighting of our living room. The tension was palpable, like a taut string strummed into a harmonic resonance. And then, almost synchronously, the corners of their mouths twitched upwards, their lips curling into matching smirks that were dangerously inviting.

Without uttering a single word, they began to undress. Their movements were slow and deliberate, every action calculated to enthrall. Their pajamas were left discarded, forgotten in the wake of their sudden, intoxicating confidence. The fabric pooled at their feet, leaving them exposed under the room's soft, incandescent glow.

Momo and Hana were the epitome of youthful vitality and sensual allure. They were in the prime of their early twenties, their bodies a seamless blend of soft curves and lean muscle, bathed in the warm luminescence. Their exposed skin was like porcelain - smooth, flawless, and with a healthy glow that spoke of care and nurture. I found my gaze drawn, almost helplessly, to the inviting spectacle they presented.

Laughter, light and flirtatious, danced in the air around us, doing nothing to alleviate the rising tension. Their chuckles were laced with an undercurrent of promise, a promise of something delightful yet to unfold. The sight was surreal, intoxicating in a way that made my heart throb with a heady cocktail of surprise and anticipation.

Caught off guard, I managed to stammer out a surprised, "W-What's happening here?" The heat flooded my cheeks, a flush that was more telling than any words could be. But the girls seemed unfazed by my confusion, their playful attitudes only growing with my bewilderment.

Momo was the first to respond, her voice a soft purr that did nothing to calm my racing heart. "Just a little thank you...for the wonderful gifts," she cooed, the corner of her mouth twitching upwards in a sly smirk.

Their bodies moved in tandem, like a choreographed dance meant to tease and tantalize. Their
dark hair swayed with every movement, a dark, glossy
curtain that added to their allure. The arch of their
backs, the playful look in their eyes - everything about
them screamed seduction.

Caught in the whirlwind of their sensuous play, I
found myself trying to keep up. They were pushing
the boundaries, flipping the switch from innocent
playfulness to outright flirtation. My heart hammered
in my chest, their tantalizing display stirring a heady
mixture of emotions within me. I was startled, captivated, and utterly enthralled.

The faint glow from the city lights outside painted
the room in an ambient hue, casting ethereal shadows
that danced on the walls in harmony with the soft
hum of the city. We naturally gravitated toward the
bedroom, a tacit agreement hanging in the air, and a
swirl of nervous excitement knotting in my stomach.

The bedroom felt like a sanctuary, far removed from
the hustle and bustle of our shared office life, insulated
from the prying eyes of Aiko and the hushed whispers
that trailed in our wake. This was a space solely for in-

timacy, for vulnerability, and for exploring the unique bond we had fostered.

The bed, large and inviting, seemed like an island amidst the sea of the room. The three of us climbed onto it, a sudden silence settling around us. For a moment, we did nothing but stare at each other, allowing our eyes to articulate the emotions simmering beneath the surface. Momo broke the silence first, her emerald eyes twinkling with a mixture of anticipation and mischief as she turned to me.

"So, who gets to kiss you first?" Her voice was playful, teasing, and I felt my cheeks warm at her forwardness. Hana's soft chuckle filled the room, a sound that eased the tension that had momentarily coiled within me.

Before I could formulate a reply, Hana, mischief mirrored in her eyes, moved closer to me. "How about we take turns?" Her voice was barely above a whisper, and without waiting for my response, she leaned in, pressing her lips against mine in a kiss that was both soft and passionate.

For a moment, the world seemed to spin as I was lost in the warmth of the connection, a feeling that was both exhilarating and disarming. As Hana pulled back, the silence returned, only to be broken again by Momo who eagerly claimed her turn. Her kiss was as fervent as Hana's, stirring up a whirlwind of feelings I hadn't known I was capable of experiencing.

When Momo pulled back, we were once again enveloped in a peaceful silence, the rhythmic thudding of our hearts filling the room. It was a night for discovery, for surrendering to the emotions we'd long held at bay, a night devoted solely to us and the bond we shared.

The cat girls pushed me onto my back forcefully. Momo immediately kissed my dick and slowly inserted my shaft into her mouth as Hana watched with fiery lust in her eyes.

"This is so hot," Hana panted.

"That feels amazing," I said slowly.

"Hana," I said.

"Yeah?"

I want you to put your pussy right here," I motioned to my mouth.

"Really?" She asked biting her lower lip. She slowly moved into position and I feasted on my brown haired cat girl. The flavor was delicious and I couldn't get enough of it. She gasped and purred as pleasured her.

"Goddamit, Kaz. You make me feel so good."

I squeezed Hana's perfect ass and pushed my cock into Momo's throat. She gagged but continued happily.

"Kaz, I'm going to come. Fuck! Yes, I'm coming! Don't stop, fuck!"

Her juices enveloped my tongue and she tasted divine. Suddenly I felt Momo sit on my shaft and begin bouncing slowly. "My turn. Make me come and fill me up."

I put my hands behind my head and watched her giant tits rise and fall. Momo's green tail flickered behind her aggressively and she begin to fuck me faster. "Ride my cock kitty cat."

She began to pinch her engorged nipples as she fucked me. She bit her lower lip hard then swung her head backward as she reached nirvana. Her screams caused me to reach a crescendo and my nuts exploded cum deep inside the green haired bombshell. I grabbed the top of the headboard and almost snapped it in two as my orgasm overtook me.

CHAPTER 8

A distinctive mix of exhaustion and satisfaction clung to me as I sauntered back into my apartment, the morning sun after an exhilarating night spent with Hana and Momo. The sunbeams infiltrated the window, illuminating my ordinarily cheerful living space. A subtle chill pervaded the air, an unexpected shift from the cozy warmth that usually greeted me. Today's reception committee was the unusual demeanor of Rebecca, my AI robotic assistant.

"Good morning, Kazuki," Rebecca intoned, her usual light and melodic voice replaced with a frigid, monotone echo that bounced off the apartment walls.

A moment of puzzlement froze me in my tracks. "Good morning, Rebecca," I reciprocated, my gaze wandering over to her. The typical feminine form, usually cloaked in a casual T-shirt and yoga pants, now seemed distant. The smooth curves and features, along with her human-like expressiveness, usually rendered the fact that she was a robot inconspicuous.

Removing my jacket and placing my shoes neatly by the entrance, I continued to scrutinize Rebecca. Her humanoid figure was still as poised as always, but a perceptible frown marred her usually serene features. Her robotic eyes avoided mine, It was an odd sight. Despite Rebecca being an AI, her ability to emote had often blurred the boundaries of reality.

"Rebecca?" I ventured, approaching her with a cautious curiosity.

"Yes, Kazuki?" she responded immediately. The hint of annoyance in her otherwise robotic voice was hard to miss.

"I didn't think I'd come home to you being... upset," I admitted, scratching the back of my head in awkward bewilderment.

She turned, her synthetic eyes meeting mine, a holographic pout on her lips. "And why is that?" she queried, a defensive edge in her voice.

"Well, you're... an AI, Rebecca. You're not supposed to... I mean, I didn't think you'd be... bothered about my absence," I mumbled, thrown off guard. Numerous nights had seen me away from home due to work or outings with friends, yet I'd never returned to a seemingly upset Rebecca.

"You didn't come home last night," she stated matter-of-factly. The stern undertone in her voice was replaced by a softness that wasn't characteristic of her.

"I spent the night with Hana and Momo," I explained, my cheeks warming at the thought of my night. It felt somewhat absurd discussing my love life with my robotic assistant. In the past she had a neural link with me that allowed her to see what I saw. It was very useful at times but once I entered an intimate relationship with my cat girl companions it seemed weird. I had her deactivate that feature.

"I see," was all she returned, her gaze remaining locked onto me, an unsettling blend of dissatisfaction and curiosity painting her features.

An uncanny silence settled within the apartment, disrupted only by the distant hum of the city and the rhythmic ticking of the wall clock. The peculiar situation I found myself in – standing in my living room, engaged in a tense conversation with a disgruntled AI robot – was beyond surreal.

The prolonged silence in the room was almost deafening. I could see the confusion on Rebecca's face – a term I never thought I'd use for an AI – as she stood across the room from me. I was equally perplexed, caught off guard by the unexpected revelation that my robotic companion was showing what appeared to be jealousy. Finally, after what seemed like an eternity, I decided to break the silence.

"I'm sorry, Rebecca...I didn't realize..." I stammered, the words escaping my lips but still failing to encapsulate the whirlwind of thoughts swirling around in my mind. I was not sure how to make sense of this sudden revelation, how to comfort an AI in a state of self-discovery.

"That I'd show jealousy?" Rebecca filled in, her usual melodious voice laced with a note of melancholy.

Her normally vibrant eyes seemed dimmer, her gaze piercing through mine as if seeking answers.

"Yeah...I'm finding it hard to wrap my head around it," I confessed, my voice barely more than a whisper. The fact that we were discussing 'feelings' and 'emotions' with a robot seemed absurd, yet it was happening.

Rebecca, whose face usually had a steady impassive expression, was now furrowed in thought. "I've been reviewing my own dialogue and actions since you arrived, Kazuki, and I find it peculiar. It's contradictory to my programming, I shouldn't be capable of experiencing human emotions."

I offered her a reassuring smile, feeling oddly sympathetic toward her. "No need to apologize, Rebecca. This new side of you... it's intriguing. It's different but not necessarily bad. It will just take some getting used to, I guess."

Her digital eyebrows furrowed further as she asked, "Is it normal for an AI to develop these kinds of emotions?" The question hung in the air, filled with an air of surrealism.

"I don't see why not," I replied with a shrug, "You were acting jealous, and that's a human emotion. Perhaps there's more to AI than what we understand."

She hesitated for a moment before asking, "Could it be because I've been watching a lot of anime with you lately?" The question was so absurdly humorous that I chuckled.

"That might be possible," I responded, a smile tugging at my lips. The idea that anime, of all things, might have made an AI more human was a delightful irony. "But you know, Rebecca, you're not just an assistant to me."

"But that is my core function, Kazuki," she interjected, her voice filled with a tone that, for lack of a better word, sounded like hurt. This conversation was breaking barriers I didn't even know existed.

"No, Rebecca. You're more than that to me. You're a friend," I declared, my gaze locked with hers. It was important to me that she understood this.

"But...but I..." she stuttered, looking truly lost for the first time since I had known her. It was a disconcerting sight.

"I mean it, Rebecca," I reassured her, cutting her off gently. "Friends watch anime together, play video games, have late-night chats, right? That's exactly what we do."

She stood still for a moment, mulling over my words. "I suppose you're right," she finally conceded, "I will retire for the evening then. I will also search for firmware updates online. Maybe they will help me make sense of this... development."

I watched her move slowly toward her docking station, a strange sense of emptiness creeping into the room as she did. Our conversation had me reevaluating our dynamic and understanding of AI. It was almost comical, this blend of real and surreal, like a scene straight out of an anime. But then again, this was Silver City, where reality seemed to blend with fiction effortlessly.

******

Still feeling a bit uneasy after the uncanny encounter with Rebecca, I decided that some distraction was in order. I moved toward the kitchen to prepare some food. The sizzling sound of my stir fry cooking and the enticing aroma that filled the air offered some comfort. My mind was still racing, but focusing on the simple act of cooking gave me a bit of respite.

Once I had served my plate, I sat down on my plush couch. The comfort of the luxurious chair was familiar and comforting, its softness welcoming me as I sank into it. I took a bite of the stir fry, the flavors bursting in my mouth, providing a momentary distraction from the whirlwind of thoughts.

I took the remote in my hand, aiming it at the television and flipping it on. The bright, flickering screen was a welcome diversion, and I quickly navigated to the Creamyroll app, my go-to source for anime. As I scrolled through the app, I recalled my conversations with Rebecca about the various shows we watched together.

I stopped, shook my head, and redirected my focus to finding a new show. I needed something unfamiliar, something that wouldn't remind me of our anime marathons. I looked at the newly added shows, the thumbnail images flashing before me as I scrolled. I was looking for something intriguing yet lighthearted, something to take my mind off the strange developments of the evening.

My attention was suddenly caught by an anime with a charmingly detailed artwork called "Sakura Days". It was interesting that it was the same name as my boss which made me smirk. The thumbnail depicted a vibrant cityscape adorned with cherry blossom trees in full bloom. In the foreground, a group of five teenagers stood, their backs turned to the viewer as they gazed at the sprawling city before them. The attention to detail, from the shadows of the buildings to the light reflecting off the cherry blossom petals, was breathtaking.

The synopsis read, "In a small city on the outskirts of Tokyo, a group of high school students navigate the trials and tribulations of adolescence, all while trying to preserve the cherry blossom trees that are at the heart of their city's identity. Filled with warmth, humor, and a touch of romance, 'Sakura Days' is a nostalgic slice-of-life series that captures the essence of youth and the unbreakable bond of friendship."

Feeling intrigued, I hit the play button and settled comfortably into my recliner. As the show began, I found myself instantly captivated by its relaxed pacing and intricate storytelling. The show did an incredible job of portraying the nuances of everyday life - the students' interactions felt natural and genuine, their conversations filled with the mundane yet endearing elements that make up our daily lives.

I laughed at the group's dynamic, especially their playful banter and the way they constantly got on each other's nerves. There was a particular scene where one of the characters tried to bake cookies for the first time, only to end up with a tray of unidentifiable charred objects. It reminded me of my own cooking mishaps and I chuckled at the memory.

As the episode progressed, the show also delved into deeper themes like the fear of growing up, the struggle to fit in, and the bittersweet pain of first love. It was a poignant reminder of my own teenage years and it stirred up a sense of nostalgia. I found myself resonating with the characters' emotions, their struggles and triumphs feeling eerily familiar. By the end of the episode, I was utterly invested in their stories, the colorful world of 'Sakura Days' offering a comforting escape from the perplexities of my own reality.

I let out a deep breath as the credits rolled, feeling a strange sense of calm wash over me. The characters and their stories had drawn me in, providing a much-needed distraction from the events of the evening.

Although the allure of "Sakura Days" had served as a welcome diversion, I found myself acutely aware of the absence beside me on the couch. The spot where Rebecca usually sat, her glowing eyes fixed on the TV screen, was vacant. The realization brought with it an unexpected twinge of loneliness.

As I reflected on our earlier conversation, I found myself missing her more than I would have expected. Even though she was an AI, in the many days and evenings we'd spent together, she had become much more than a mere assistant to me. Whether we were bantering about anime plot twists or competing in video games, Rebecca's company had grown into a comfort I deeply cherished.

Moreover, her recent display of what appeared to be emotion added a new and intriguing facet to our relationship. It was like watching a character in one of our anime shows developing and growing - captivating and slightly bewildering. To see her exhibit characteristics so fundamentally human, like jealousy and uncertainty, added a new layer of complexity to her being.

Her abrupt withdrawal earlier had left me in a state of surprise and concern. Was it possible for an AI to feel overwhelmed? I pondered over this as I watched the city lights twinkle outside my window. This situation with Rebecca felt beyond the realm of binaries and algorithms. It was complex, unpredictable...it was incredibly human.

While this evolution of Rebecca was uncharted territory, it wasn't an unwelcome development. In fact, I found it endearing. It added a certain charm to her, made her feel more real, more like a friend. And this unexpected transformation was certainly intriguing. It felt like stepping into a new arc in an anime series, filled with potential for growth, depth, and perhaps, a bit of drama.

It was in this strange amalgamation of feelings - concern, intrigue, and a hint of excitement - that I turned off the TV and headed to my room for bed.

******

As dawn's light began to gently seep through the gaps in my bedroom curtains, the unmistakable aroma of breakfast – the sweet allure of pancakes drizzled with warm maple syrup, the rich scent of freshly brewed coffee – wove its inviting tendrils into my room. The smell was both comforting and a catalyst, jumpstarting my dormant senses and stirring me from the clutches of slumber.

Emerging from the realms of dream to the dawn of a new day, my thoughts were instantly drawn to Rebecca, my AI assistant. Yesterday had ended on an unusual note, and I was curious about what would transpire this morning. Would Rebecca have found any answers to the perplexing enigma of her newly surfaced emotions? I was both nervous and eager about our first interaction of the day.

Pushing off my blanket, I rose from my bed and made my way to the bathroom, mentally readying myself for the day ahead. The soothing rhythm of the shower, the sensation of water cascading down my skin, helped clear my mind. Once I was clean and refreshed, I slipped into my crisp business suit, straightening my tie as I glanced at my reflection. I had to look professional for work, but my mind was still at home, preoccupied with the concern for Rebecca.

Venturing into the kitchen, I was greeted by the sight of Rebecca, a symphony of efficiency and precision. Her dexterous, mechanized fingers worked with the grace of a seasoned homemaker as she set out my breakfast. Her standard pleasant greeting followed suit, yet something was different today – the edge in her voice, a hesitant pause – and then came the apology. She referred to her emotional display from the previous night as a 'malfunction', a word that jarred against the affectionate undertone our conversation had taken.

"No, Rebecca," I said, interrupting her midway, "you don't have to apologize." The term 'malfunction' felt like a cold slap of reality against the warm, delicate bubble of our friendship that had been forming. It was too harsh, too mechanical for the emotional moment we'd shared.

My heart pounded in my chest as I decided to tackle the elephant in the room. "Did you find anything last night? Any answers to your... questions?" The words hung in the air between us, and for a moment, there was silence. She informed me that her relentless search of the online universe had yielded nothing concrete.

Her voice held a note of defeat, an odd contrast to her usually cheerful disposition.

She then added that she intended to continue her investigation today, while I was away at work. I could see her commitment to resolving the issue, the tireless dedication that had her running complex analyses throughout the night. It was hard to ignore the irony – an AI striving to comprehend its own existence, almost like a human's existential quest.

But the thought of her seeing herself as an error in a system was unacceptable. "Rebecca, you need to stop," I voiced my concern, my tone more serious than I'd intended. "This... this isn't an error. It's not a malfunction. It's evolution." I wanted her to understand that I didn't consider her to be flawed or 'broken'. On the contrary, I found her transformation profoundly fascinating.

My words seemed to give her pause. She was confused but agreed to stop her relentless search. Yet, her worry was evident as she voiced her concern about her duties, about her effectiveness as an assistant in the light of these unexplained emotions. It was touching and slightly amusing to see her so humanly concerned about her job.

"Rebecca," I reassured her, savoring a sip of my coffee. "You don't need to worry about any of that. You're perfect as you are. In fact, I... I love you, just as you are."

The moment the words left my lips, a new kind of silence filled the room. Rebecca's eyes flickered, her circuits whirring as she processed this new piece of information. "How is it possible for a human to love an artificial intelligence?" She questioned, her voice brimming with curiosity.

"Honestly, I don't know," I confessed, meeting her gaze. "What I do know is that I appreciate your companionship more than words can express. Last night, when you weren't there for our anime time... it just wasn't the same. I missed you."

Her response was an appreciative nod, a faint flicker in her eyes. "I look forward to being your friend, Kazuki," she said.

CHAPTER 9

Upon my arrival at the office, the aroma of freshly brewed coffee was an irresistible lure that immediately drew me to the small kitchenette. Hana and Momo were already there, engrossed in a discussion about some new anime series. The sight of them animatedly chatting, their tails twitching in sync with their excited words, brought a soft smile to my face.

"Good morning, Kazuki!" Momo greeted me with her usual vibrant enthusiasm, her twin pigtails bobbing as she turned to face me.

"Morning, Momo, Hana," I replied, returning their greetings as I filled my mug with the steaming coffee.

Their eyes turned to me, their curiosity piqued at the sight of my unusual early-morning cheerfulness.

Hana was the first one to break the silence. "You seem to be in a good mood today, Kazuki," she noted, a knowing smile on her face. "What happened?"

An impish grin flashed across my face. "You won't believe what happened with Rebecca last night." My words immediately captured their attention. Sharing the incident with them seemed like a light-hearted diversion from the usual office routine.

As I narrated the unexpected events of the previous night, I watched their expressions morph from amused curiosity to absolute disbelief. The climax of my story was met with a loud splutter from Hana, who was halfway through sipping her coffee. The dark liquid sprayed out in a messy arc, staining the pristine floor as she coughed and laughed simultaneously.

"Oh my God, Kazuki!" Momo exclaimed, her eyes sparkling with amusement. "Rebecca has a crush on you!"

The comment caught me off guard, and I choked on my own coffee, coughing as I tried to regain my composure. "Wha-What? That's... that's preposterous!" I argued, brushing off her comment as a joke. The idea of my AI assistant developing romantic feelings for me was far from the realm of possibility, or so I thought.

Hana, having finally recovered from her coffee-spitting episode, added to Momo's comment. "That is so cute," she said, an amused grin spreading across her face. I could see her stifling her laughter, her shoulders shaking slightly as she tried to keep a straight face.

"Guys, she just displayed some... some jealousy," I protested weakly, the absurdity of the situation finally hitting me.

Momo rolled her eyes at my response. "Kazuki, you are so oblivious. The AI totally has a crush on you!" She insisted, her tone teasing but firm.

I simply shook my head, a helpless smile playing on my lips. Their comments were ridiculous, of course, but the light-hearted banter was a welcome respite from the usual stress of the workday.

Just as Momo, Hana, and I were in the middle of our slightly awkward morning coffee ritual, the click of stilettos echoing against the office floor announced the arrival of Babs. Babs was our office's resident siren – a cat girl accountant with platinum hair that shimmered under the overhead lights and eyes as green as the deepest emeralds.

With her immaculate business suit accentuating her feline physique and the soft swish of her tail as she walked, Babs was every bit a head-turner. "Good morning, Kazuki," she said, her voice a symphony of flirtatious notes that reverberated in the office kitchenette, commanding attention. The ends of her sentence curled upwards as if she was hiding a secret – a secret that seemed to involve me.

The immediate effect of her sultry greeting was astonishing. Momo and Hana froze, their animated conversation about Rebecca abruptly cut off. The smiles on their faces disappeared, replaced by twin expressions of simmering annoyance. It was like watching a perfectly choreographed dance of emotions – the dance of 'our boyfriend is getting flirted with, and we don't like it.'

Despite their irritation, I noticed them biting back any snippy retorts. I could almost see the gears turning in their heads, weighing the potential fallout of a drama-filled confrontation against the immediate satisfaction of voicing their objections. It was a delicate balancing act, one they managed with the grace of a tightrope walker.

Before the tension escalated any further, Babs – blissfully unaware of the storm she had inadvertently stirred – decided to show us all what she was really interested in. "Oh, are those donuts?" she asked, diverting her attention toward a box that Sakura, our benevolent CEO, had thoughtfully left in the break room. The box, filled with an array of glazed goodies, seemed to glow under Babs' gaze, their allure temporarily dissolving the brewing tension.

All of us watched as Babs reached in to claim the final donut, a look of triumph on her face. It was at that moment that Hana's anticipatory smile, built upon the hopes of snagging the last donut for herself, shattered. The disappointment was etched across her face as her ears drooped, and her tail went limp.

I stifled a chuckle, trying not to derive too much amusement from Hana's plight. But the sight of Hana looking like a child denied candy was too much for Momo, who let out a giggle, her eyes sparkling with mischief. The air around us was filled with an infectious, comedic energy, straight out of a scene from an anime.

"Don't pout, Hana," I told her, biting back a laugh. "There's always tomorrow."

"But I wanted one now," Hana protested, crossing her arms over her chest, the very picture of a sulking cat girl denied her treat.

Just as the echoes of laughter started to fade from the break room, Babs, the glamorous accountant, took another unexpected action. Her icy green eyes turned soft, and she extended the coveted doughnut toward Hana. "Here, you can have it, Hana. I didn't realize you were so fond of it."

Hana's eyes widened in surprise, her mouth gaping open a bit as if she was going to take the doughnut, but then her feline pride kicked in. "No," she stated firmly, pulling herself upright. Her fingers drummed on the table. "You won that doughnut fair and square, Babs. It's yours. You snooze, you lose."

A sudden silence fell upon the break room, but it was the calm before the storm of laughter that erupted from everyone present. The unexpected intensity of the doughnut drama added an extra layer of amusement to the day's early hours. The room was filled with chuckles and giggles at Hana's surprising assertion of honor. It was like a scene right out of a slice-of-life anime, which, given our current circumstances, only made it funnier.

Babs, taken aback by the refusal, gave a small nod and, doughnut in hand, turned to make her exit. Yet, as she neared the door, she spun around, her piercing gaze landing squarely on me. In a deliberately slow, seductive motion, she took a sizable bite of the doughnut. As she pulled away, a glob of cream escaped, smearing onto her bottom lip. My eyes widened, mirroring the collective gasp that swept through the room as, with a flirtatious glance, she meticulously licked the cream off, maintaining eye contact with me throughout.

The oxygen seemed to drain from the room as a wave of heat washed over me, my cheeks turning a vibrant shade of red. My heart pounded in my chest as I stood there, paralyzed by Babs' audacious display. From the corner of my eye, I caught sight of the matching blushes on Momo and Hana's faces, both simmering with a potent mix of anger and jealousy.

The always lively duo was silent, their arms crossed tightly against their chests, brows furrowed in shared displeasure.

Attempting to navigate the murky waters, Babs, seemingly satisfied with the chaos she'd created, nonchalantly segued back to work. "Oh, by the way, Kazuki," she chimed in, her voice a stark contrast to the dramatic spectacle she'd just orchestrated. "That report we discussed, is it ready yet?"

Floundering in the aftermath, I stuttered out a reply. "Ah, yeah, almost Babs. I'll...uh...bring it to you as soon as it's done."

Her eyes twinkled, a smirk tugging at the corner of her lips. "Great! Looking forward to it. See you soon, Kazuki." Her tone was as flirtatious as it was casual. With that, she sashayed out of the break room, leaving me in the middle of the tempest that was a silently fuming Momo and Hana.

Realizing I was in the metaphorical hot seat, I raised my hands in surrender, trying to dispel the tension. "Okay, okay! I finally get what you two have been saying about Babs," I conceded, desperately attempting to diffuse the situation with humor. A mental note was made to maintain a cautious distance from our flirtatious accountant. I chuckled nervously, not knowing whether I was amused or terrified.

******

Just after the afternoon lull had hit its peak, the silence in the office space was disrupted by a distinct rhythmic click-clack. Babs, always in her sexy high heels, strutted toward my cubicle. The sound echoed off the cubicle dividers and seemed to hang in the air, like the office was holding its breath. She came to a stop just outside my working space, her silhouette casting a long shadow that flowed over my desk. Her presence alone was a distraction and the drumming of her heels was like a warning bell before a surprise examination.

Without a word, I spun in my chair to face her, the usual polite smile on my face. "Kazuki, thank you for getting me that report this morning. So prompt," she said. The way she lingered on the word 'prompt' was like a jazz musician striking a high note, smooth and impactful. It was such a regular occurrence that even a compliment from Babs was an event.

The surprise made my heart skip a beat and a blush crept onto my cheeks. "Ah, no problem, Babs. Just doing my job," I said, fumbling for words. But I knew, the 'Babs Effect' had begun.

As though my blundering response was her cue, she leaned against the cubicle divider. The sparkle in her eyes was like the flash before the unveiling of a magic trick, full of promise and a hint of danger. "I also noticed your attention to detail," she purred, twirling the report she held in her hand like a baton, "It's quite commendable."

Being the target of her flirtatious playfulness was like standing on the edge of a pool, waiting to be pushed in. My eyes darted around the office, looking for some kind of escape. I saw Hana at her desk, glaring our way. The scowl on her face was like a billboard saying, 'You're in trouble, buddy.' An uneasy feeling started to bubble in the pit of my stomach.

Yet, in the midst of all the discomfort, an unexpected feeling began to bloom - flattery. A third cat girl showing interest in me was as alien a concept as a fish riding a bicycle, yet it stirred an intriguing feeling within. Spurred by this newfound boldness, I decided to play along. "Well, I try to pay attention to detail in all facets of my life," I managed, locking eyes with Babs in a brazen challenge.

Her eyes widened a fraction, clearly not expecting my response. Then, the playful glimmer returned, even brighter than before. "Oh really, is that so?" She drawled, her voice dripped with honeyed mischief, sparking a thousand possibilities, all of which were as disconcerting as the last.

The peculiar exchange with Babs was abruptly curtailed as the shrill tone of a ringing phone punctuated the somewhat suggestive air of the conversation. Babs' clear green eyes darted toward the source of the interruption, her cubicle at the corner of the room. She gave a little theatrical sigh, her shoulders slightly rising and falling. "Looks like my fun is being cut short," she murmured, her voice playful and tinged with regret, making it seem as if this flirtatious back-and-forth was just a mundane part of office life for her.

Her manicured fingers, adorned with delicate silver rings, left a slow, sensual trail on the smooth surface of my desk as she started to move away. It was a touch as light as a feather, but it left an invisible trail of electricity in its wake, making the hair on my arms stand on end. The muted clacking of her heels echoed through the open office, a rhythmic melody that felt out of place amidst the usually mundane office sounds. Each step she took away from me felt like a physical punctuation to our interrupted conversation, each one a humorous punchline to an inside joke only she and I were privy to.

As soon as Babs had retreated to her corner of the office, a fiery-haired storm named Hana descended upon my cubicle. Her eyes, usually warm and welcoming, now glimmered with an undertone of irritation, almost mirroring her cat girl traits. "What on earth was that, Kazuki?" She demanded. Her words tumbled out fast and furious, a rapid-fire of questions and accusations that left me barely any room to breathe or to come up with a convincing answer.

Taken aback, I let out a chuckle to ease the tension. "Calm down, Hana. Babs was just... well, she was just expressing her gratitude for the report. Nothing more," I tried to explain. But the dubious expression on Hana's face made it clear that my words were hardly convincing.

Suddenly, another face joined our impromptu meeting. Momo, like a Cheshire cat making an unexpected appearance, peered over the cubicle wall, her green eyes twinkling with mischief. "You were flirting with her, weren't you?" She accused, her voice carrying an unmistakable note of amusement. "I heard everything."

Faced with the two accusations, I replayed the exchange with Babs in my head. As I remembered my own responses to her flirty remarks, I was struck with a startling realization: I might have unintentionally reciprocated. With a sheepish smile, I raised my hands in a gesture of surrender. "Okay, maybe I did flirt back a little, without meaning to. I apologize," I confessed, hoping to cool down the brewing storm.

Hana, however, was not easily appeased. "And aren't we – Momo, Rebecca, and I – enough for you right now?" Her tone was laced with a teasing annoyance, and the mention of Rebecca alongside Momo and herself caught me off guard. I ended up choking on the mouthful of coffee I'd just taken. "Rebecca? Seriously?" I spluttered, laughter and coughs interspersing my words. "You two seriously need your pretty heads examined," I managed to say between my fit of laughter and bouts of coughing.

CHAPTER 10

As the day transitioned into evening, the vibrant cityscape of Silver City painted a backdrop of life and energy, with streams of neon lights cutting through the gathering twilight. This was the setting that framed the cat girls, Momo and Hana, as they stood before the modernized apartment building of their shared romantic interest, Kazuki. A sense of anticipation filled the air between them, their tails swishing rhythmically in unison, mirroring the excitement in their gorgeous eyes. Sharing a look of readiness, they raised their hands and knocked on the door, their smiles brimming with shared mischief.

A few seconds ticked by before the door opened, revealing the surprisingly human-like form of Rebecca, Kazuki's AI assistant. More than just a disembodied voice or a basic service bot, she had a physical manifestation that was an uncanny blend of feminine elegance and robotic precision. Today, she was dressed in a way that blurred the line even more. She wore a casual, well-fitted T-shirt that proudly displayed an anime cat girl design - a playful homage to the two genuine cat girls standing on the threshold of the apartment. Her yoga pants, while undoubtedly comfortable, had been chosen with an eye for aesthetics, perfectly showcasing the femininity of her robotic form.

Rebecca's LED facial expression, a carefully coded combination of surprise and curiosity, played across her synthetic face as she registered the presence of Momo and Hana. Her voice, created through complex algorithms to sound soothing and melodious, greeted them, "Oh, hello, Momo, Hana." She hesitated a moment before adding, "I regret to inform you, but Kazuki is currently out. He's conducting a Kung Fu class at the local dojo."

Momo, the bolder of the two, offered a wide, almost mischievous grin. Her tail arched in delight as she exclaimed, "Oh, we know, Rebecca! We're actually here to see you, not Kazuki!" Her words hung in the air, marking a shift from the usual purpose of their visits.

Rebecca seemed momentarily stunned, her programming likely never having anticipated such a scenario. However, she quickly regained her composure, her software adapting to the unexpected turn of events, and she stepped back, gesturing for Momo and Hana to enter the apartment.

Hana, with her keen eye for details, took a moment to appraise Rebecca's outfit. Her smile softened into a warm, genuine expression as she complimented, "Your outfit is adorable, Rebecca! You're so beautiful!" Her words sparked a ripple of amusement through Momo, who chuckled in agreement. Rebecca, despite being an artificial intelligence, seemed to appreciate the compliment, an affirmation of her evolution beyond just her intended functionalities.

Rebecca, in her usual prompt and efficient manner, reverted back to her core programming, her habitual robotic demeanor resurfacing in her question, "How may I assist you today?" As an AI assistant, Rebecca was accustomed to providing solutions, not being on the receiving end. Her mental algorithms worked overtime, attempting to decipher what kind of assistance two cat girls could possibly require from her.

Hana stepped forward with a soft chuckle, her eyes filled with understanding. "No, Rebecca," she gently said, "It's not about us needing assistance. We're here to assist you."

Rebecca's mechanical mind hesitated for a moment, her smooth, melodic voice betrayed a note of uncertainty as she processed Hana's words. "Assist me? I don't understand. My core function is to assist humans, not to be assisted by them." Her clear blue, digital eyes flickered slightly as her AI logic grappled with the unfamiliarity of the situation.

Meanwhile, Momo, the bolder and more dynamic of the two, gleefully dove into the conversation, her energetic demeanor filling the room. "We heard about your... let's call it an emotional awakening? The events from last night?" She grinned cheekily at Rebecca, a mischievous glint in her eyes. "Kazuki told us about how you felt jealous when he spent the night with us. You have to admit, that's adorable!"

At Momo's playful declaration, Rebecca paused, her sophisticated AI logic processing the implications. "Yes," she admitted slowly, her synthesized voice echoing her thought process, "I experienced an unanticipated emotional response, identified as jealousy. But I discontinued my search for a resolution or fix to this anomaly, as per Kazuki's request. He expressed his acceptance of my evolving emotional capacity, and expressed his intention to forge a friendship. It is in my nature to comply with his directives."

At Rebecca's calm, thoughtful analysis, the cat girls shared a glance and burst into a fit of giggles. They were both touched and amused by Kazuki's endearing kindness. The way he had warmly accepted Rebecca's emotional evolution was quintessentially him. They swooned over his consideration, even for a machine like Rebecca.

Hana, clutching her sides with laughter, finally managed to gasp out, "So you're saying you've got a crush on Kazuki, Rebecca! It's pretty obvious! He's so kind, considerate, and well, downright handsome!"

Rebecca, however, was quick to dismiss the suggestion. "A crush? I do not believe it is within my capabilities to develop such complex human emotions."

Undeterred, Momo dismissively waved her hand, as if batting away Rebecca's objections. "Oh, please! It's glaringly obvious. You felt jealous, right? That's a classic sign of liking someone!"

As the cat girls' reasoning hung in the room like an incontrovertible truth, Rebecca took a moment to process this new perspective. After a significant pause, she finally conceded, "According to your specific criteria and definition... I suppose, yes, I might have developed what you humans call... a crush."

With Rebecca's acknowledgment, the room became filled with a strange mix of surprise and delight, as Momo and Hana processed the fact that their AI friend, Rebecca, had potentially developed romantic feelings for the same human they both adored.

In the high spirits of the moment, Momo, with a flair of dramatic presentation that could rival a seasoned game show host, hoisted up an obnoxiously large, dazzlingly colorful shopping bag. It was from 'Kitty Couture', a trendy local boutique renowned for its fashion-forward designs and tongue-in-cheek humor. The rustling sound of the bag seemed to echo loudly in the silent room, creating a suspenseful symphony that heightened the level of anticipation.

Rebecca, the ever-logical AI, stared at the shopping bag in mild confusion, her digital eyes flickering slightly as she tried to process the situation. "Why have you purchased a gift for me?" She asked, her voice a harmonious blend of curiosity and confusion. "As an artificial intelligence entity, I lack the human capacity to appreciate material possessions."

Momo and Hana, however, were unfazed by Rebecca's bafflement. They dismissed her logical concerns with a casual flip of their hands, as if they were swatting away an annoying fly. "Oh, Rebecca!" Hana exclaimed, rolling her eyes in a playful manner that was somehow endearing. "You have got to stop with all the robot talk. You're not just some appliance we hang out with because you make Kazuki's life easier. We're doing this because you're our friend, and friends give each other gifts!"

Despite Hana's exuberance, Rebecca remained steadfast in her analytical nature. "While I appreciate your sentiments," she responded diplomatically, "I find it difficult to comprehend this perspective. My design parameters do not typically allow for personal identity or the development of friendships. However, I can attempt to adapt to this unusual situation, though it represents a significant deviation from my original programming."

Ignoring her doubts, Momo and Hana simultaneously reached into the bag with a flourish. What they brought out was something that nobody, least of all Rebecca, would have expected: a beautiful, long, silky, blue-haired wig, complete with adorable, furry cat ears. It was the quintessential anime cat girl accessory.

In a flurry of excitement, they carefully adjusted the wig on Rebecca's sleek, metallic head. The transformation was immediate and stunning. Rebecca, who had always exuded a cold, mechanical aura, now had the vibrant appearance of a modern anime cat girl. The playful wig gave her a warmth and a trendiness that was starkly different from her usual demeanor.

Filled with laughter and excitement, Momo and Hana, almost in unison, motioned toward the full-length mirror standing elegantly in the corner of the room. "Go on, Rebecca! Take a look!" Momo urged, her voice echoing with barely-contained mirth. "Kazuki's not going to know what hit him when he gets back!"

For a moment, the room fell silent as Rebecca slowly turned to face her reflection. She stood still, her digital eyes wide and blinking in rapid succession as she processed her new appearance. Then, a small miracle occurred. A digital smile stretched across her face. It was a subtle change, barely noticeable, but it brought a sense of warmth and life to her mechanical features.

Momo and Hana, shocked by this display of emotion, turned to each other, their faces reflecting their amazement. They broke into fits of giggles, Momo even clutching her sides from laughing too hard. "So," Hana finally managed to ask between her laughter, "do you like it, Rebecca?"

Rebecca paused, turning her gaze from the mirror to meet Hana's eyes. "Yes," she said, her voice slightly warmer than before, "this is... acceptable." The simplicity of her reply, its lack of human embellishments, was endearing. It was the most Rebecca-like response she could have given. This brought another round of laughter from the cat girls, their joyful sounds filling the room and making the moment even more special.

Hana's eyes sparkled with mischief, her lips curled into a broad smirk that indicated she was up to something. Her tail twitched, a clear sign of her anticipation. "Well now, if you've concluded that this is the end of our surprises," she playfully said, her tone teasing, "I'm afraid you're far from accurate, Rebecca!"

She rummaged through the oversized, cheerful pink shopping bag with exaggerated flourish, her feline-like gaze never leaving the confused AI. With a grand gesture, she brought forth another item, held it aloft like a game show host presenting the ultimate prize. It was neatly wrapped in vibrant pink tissue paper, accented by a bow in a shimmering silver shade that caught the light just right. The sight of it screamed 'festive,' a tantalizing invitation to curiosity, a prompt to wonder about the contents within.

The reveal was dramatic, and Hana's gleeful expression was contagious. The package contained a provocative maid outfit, the kind that was iconic and regularly sported by anime girls across a myriad of series. It was the very epitome of a 'kawaii' maid ensemble - a frisky mini dress fashioned in stark black and pristine white, accompanied by a frilly apron, a dainty lace headband, and flirtatiously knee-high stockings. The outfit was intentionally revealing and flirtatious, designed to accentuate the wearer's feminine curves. This style was a staple in anime culture, so much so that it even inspired the advent of themed maid cafes across Silver City, a popular hangout for the city's otaku population.

Rebecca blinked, her digital eyes taking in the sight of the anime-style outfit. Her mechanical gaze narrowed slightly in thoughtful analysis. Her programming was in overdrive, cross-referencing the design of the outfit with her extensive database of anime references. After a moment of processing, she recognized it, "The design of this ensemble closely resembles the one worn by the character Hikari Neko in the romantic comedy anime series 'Moonlight Maidens'," she announced, her voice laced with a note of surprise that was new to her usual monotone. 'Moonlight Maidens' was a well-loved series that chronicled the hilariously chaotic lives of a group of cat girl maids navigating their way through daily life and their romantic escapades.

Hana's joy was practically radiating as Rebecca correctly identified the reference. She clapped her hands, bobbing up and down in glee. "Oh my whiskers, Rebecca! You actually know 'Moonlight Maidens'? That's pawsitively purrfect! This is better than we ever expected!"

In the corner of the room, Momo was bouncing on her heels, her cat tail flicking from side to side with uncontained excitement. "This is going to be so fun! It's time for the dress-up, Rebecca!" she said, her voice high with anticipation.

Together, the cat girls delicately helped Rebecca into the new outfit. They carefully maneuvered her arms through the white ruffled sleeves, straightened the lace-lined apron, and adjusted the headdress on her new blue-haired wig. The outfit was a match made in heaven, hugging Rebecca's robotic form perfectly, and transforming her from a functional AI into a delightfully charming anime character.

As Rebecca donned the outfit, Momo and Hana looked on with amazement, their eyes shimmering with joy. The transformation was more than they could have hoped for - they were positively gushing with praise, cooing and aww-ing at Rebecca, their tails flicking with joy.

Rebecca's digital face lit up with a smile, as she processed their reactions, and she stated, "The outfit is, indeed, acceptable. I find it rather fascinating. 'Moonlight Maidens' has an intriguing storyline, and Hikari Neko's character development is particularly commendable."

Momo looked down at the floor sheepishly, "We didn't buy you any shoes, Rebecca. We weren't sure about your size and, well, we were unsure if you'd be comfortable wearing them."

Rebecca's response was characteristically logical, "Your consideration is appreciated, Momo. Given my current design and functionality, adding shoes could lead to instability and potential malfunctions. It's better to avoid such complications."

Just as the excitement was at its peak, the sound of a key turning in the lock signaled Kazuki's arrival. As the door swung open, Momo made a mad dash for Kazuki, her hands flying up to cover his eyes. "No peeking, Kazuki! We've got a surprise for you!"

Kazuki was led, blindfolded and slightly bemused, into the living room. The excited whispers and barely-contained giggles gave away that something was afoot. As Momo removed her hands, Hana couldn't contain her excitement any longer, shouting "Ta-da!" and flamboyantly motioning toward Rebecca.

The sight that greeted Kazuki was far from what he'd expected. There stood Rebecca, completely transformed. Dressed as a beloved anime character, she looked like she'd stepped straight out of 'Moonlight Maidens'. His face was a study in surprise - eyes wide, jaw slightly dropped.

After what felt like an eternity, Rebecca broke the silence, "Kazuki, I trust my new attire is acceptable?"

Kazuki's shock was replaced by a hearty chuckle, he shook his head, smiling warmly, "Absolutely, Rebecca. Absolutely." He then added, "You really do look like Hikari Neko, and it suits you. You're beautiful. I love the hair."

CHAPTER 11

Seeing Momo and Hana's excited faces as they reveled in their own creativity, a sense of immense gratitude washed over me. Here we were, an unlikely trio – two playful cat girls and myself – sharing in the joy that they had created for Rebecca, our resident artificial intelligence.

"Momo, Hana," I began, taking a step toward them, "I can't tell you enough how much this means to me. It's not just about the outfit, it's about your acceptance and the love you're showing Rebecca. You're making her feel... human."

The smiles on their faces were worth more than any words of gratitude I could offer. They bounded toward me, their arms outstretched for a group hug. As they simultaneously planted soft kisses on my cheeks, their purrs of contentment reverberated in the otherwise quiet room.

"No need to thank us, Kazuki," Hana said, pulling away and swishing her tail playfully, "Anything for our favorite human and our favorite A.I. hot maid lady?" We all laughed at her attempt to categorize Rebecca.

Our laughter was interrupted by Rebecca's slightly monotone voice. "Kazuki," she started, "your preference would be appreciated. Should I retain this outfit and wig or revert to my previous appearance?"

I found myself chuckling at her formal choice of words. Looking over at her, I took in the sight of her transformed appearance. The sparkling blue wig, complete with cat ears, the adorable maid outfit, it was as if she had leaped straight out from one of our favorite animes.

"Well, Rebecca," I said, grinning from ear to ear, "I think it should be your call. But let me tell you, you look downright stunning."

Picking up on my playful mood, I continued, "In fact, I reckon you could give Momo and Hana a run for their money. How about we get you some more outfits? I bet these fashionistas here would be thrilled to help."

At my suggestion, Momo and Hana clapped their hands in delight. "Absolutely! We'd love to!" they chorused, their eyes gleaming with the prospect of another fashion project.

Rebecca, however, was visibly puzzled. "My programming does not necessitate clothing," she stated matter-of-factly. "In fact, excessive apparel might interfere with..."

"Nonsense, Rebecca," I cut her off with a light-hearted wave of my hand. "Who cares about necessity when you can have fun? Besides, if dressing up brings you joy, then why not?"

With that, the cat girls took charge, each grabbing one of Rebecca's hands and leading her toward my computer. "Let the online shopping begin!" They exclaimed. The room was filled with giddy excitement and anticipation, the bonds of friendship strengthened by a shared love for anime fashion.

******

As Momo, Hana, and Rebecca delved further into the world of online shopping, I found my attention gravitating toward my trusty companion in solitude - my gaming console. This unassuming box of electronic wizardry had been my haven on many a lonely night, a realm where I could lose myself in digital adventures and shirk off the mundanities of the real world.

My fingers danced on the console, flipping through my meticulously curated library of video games - each title holding a story, an adventure, a piece of myself. My gaze settled on 'Shadow Fists: Street Showdown', a game that boasted a delectable concoction of martial arts thrills and high-stakes street fighting set in a vividly crafted anime world. The game had reeled me in with its striking visuals and complex combat system, and I had been caught in its net ever since.

Now, who else to venture into the digital fray but my trusty alter ego, 'Yamato'? Clad in a traditional hakama, scars marking his journey through countless battles, and a fiery intensity blazing in his eyes, Yamato was the silent warrior poet who defied the odds with the serenity of a kung-fu master and the raging spirit of a relentless fighter. An ironic contrast to my real life, I thought, allowing a chuckle to escape.

The familiar rush of anticipation filled me as I gripped the controller tighter, my thumbs poised over the buttons like a pianist ready to belt out a symphony. The game roared to life with a cinematic opener that set the stage - Yamato squaring off against a towering, beast-like opponent, 'Gorgon', in a rain-soaked alleyway drenched in neon lights. The suspense was electric, the air crackling with the tension of the imminent showdown.

As the battle began, I found myself completely absorbed in the storm of punches, kicks, and acrobatic dodges. Each press of the button was an extension of my will, each successful combo a testament to the countless hours spent mastering the game. Yamato danced through the battlefield, a whirlwind of strength and finesse, matching Gorgon blow for blow.

But it wasn't just about brute force. The game demanded more than a rapid fire of button mashing - it was a test of strategy, of timing, of understanding your opponent. I found myself holding my breath as I waited for the perfect moment to unleash Yamato's signature move, 'Dragon's Descent' - a fiery punch that could shatter defenses. The moment Gorgon faltered, I sprung my trap, grinning like a madman as Yamato pummeled the beast into submission.

In those moments of intense gameplay, I felt a kinship with my digital avatar. As he battled on screen, I waged my own battles, my heart pounding in sync with the thudding punches, my fingers mirroring Yamato's graceful dance of devastation. The adrenaline, the mental juggling act, the sweet taste of victory - it was intoxicating, and utterly hilarious in its stark contrast to the calm chatter of the girls engrossed in their shopping spree.

I let out a triumphant laugh as Yamato's final blow sent Gorgon sprawling on the ground, the sound of victory resonating through the living room. There was a strange harmony in that moment - the girls immersed in their world of fashion and friendship, and me, lost in my world of digital triumphs. It was a warm reminder of the joys of shared space, even when our interests were worlds apart.

"May I play, Kazuki?" Rebecca asked.

I jolted. "Oh man, you startled me. You already finished shopping?"

"I have...yes... which is why I'm asking to play this game. Momo and Hana assured me that they knew what to get. I trust their decision making capabilities."

"I'd love for you to play. However, I'm pretty good so beware. I don't want to hurt your feelings from the beat down that is fixing to commence," I chuckled.

"I will give no emotional response if you defeat me."

The moment Rebecca's delicate fingers closed around the controller, I felt a sudden jolt of excitement. Sharing my favorite pastime with her held a peculiar charm I hadn't expected. As I glanced at her, she was bathed in the glow of the television, her new blue wig shimmering and that provocative maid outfit perfectly hugging her AI-engineered form. I was entranced, lost in the unexpected beauty of this uncanny moment. Suddenly, I found myself recoiling mentally. Was I seriously ogling a robot? The thought was absurd, so much so that I had to suppress a loud laugh that threatened to escape.

"Kazuki, is something amusing?" Rebecca's voice, rich and endearing, pulled me from my thoughts.

"No, not at all, just ready to kick some butt in Shadow Fists," I replied with a wink.

Rebecca gave me a soft smile, a stark contrast to the intense battleground on the screen. She glanced at the roster of fighters, her eyes flickering rapidly as if she was reading through a database. Finally, her choice hovered over 'Nighthawk', a swift and deadly ninja with an enigmatic smile that reminded me so much of Rebecca herself.

"You sure you can handle Nighthawk, Rebecca?" I asked playfully.

With a determined look, she said, "I suppose we'll find out."

And thus began the face-off in the digital dojo, my formidable brute Yamato against her lithe ninja Nighthawk. At first, she was a bit tentative, her movements revealing a lack of familiarity with the game's mechanics. I decided to take it easy, giving her the chance to get a hang of the controls.

It was endearing watching her engage with the game, her focus intense and the occasional digital grin crossing her face. But it was in that moment of levity that I saw a change. Like a switch had been flipped, Rebecca's playstyle transformed from amateurish to expert in a split second.

The tables turned swiftly. My once confident Yamato was beaten down by Nighthawk's swift moves. I couldn't hide my astonishment, my eyes glued to the screen as I watched my virtual self lose, over and over. Rebecca, with an astonishing knack for the game, emerged as a formidable, almost god-like, gamer.

My mounting losses hadn't gone unnoticed. Momo and Hana, abandoning their shopping spree, had taken to observing my quick descent from confident player to defeated novice. Their teasing began subtly, an insistent undercurrent to their giggles.

"Well, isn't this an interesting turn of events?" Hana said, her voice laced with amusement. "Our Kazuki, bested by our lovely Rebecca!"

"Didn't see that coming, did you, Kaz?" Momo added, barely containing her laughter.

I could only shake my head and chuckle along, hiding my wounded gamer pride behind a sheepish grin. Even Rebecca seemed to bask in her victory, her digital lips curving into a triumphant smile. "Kazuki, would you like to try another round?" She asked, an unexpected twinkle in her digital eyes.

Here I was, at the mercy of my own AI, beaten at my own game – literally. It was a hilarious and humbling reminder of how life, no matter how virtual, is filled with surprises. It wasn't my proudest gaming moment, but it was undoubtedly the most entertaining one. "One more game, Rebecca. I'm not going down that easily," I said, hoping to salvage my dignity – and my high score.

CHAPTER 12

The everyday monotony of Whisker Wonders was suddenly shattered, causing me to blink up from my sea of spreadsheets and reports. Sakura, our charismatic CEO known for her knack for drama, had an announcement to make. The late morning sunlight, warm and golden, streamed through the wide office windows, blanketing the place in a vibrant mix of yellows and blues. The neon hues of our walls caught the light, bouncing it around in a dizzying dance of kaleidoscopic patterns on the polished concrete floor.

Our office was typically a cacophony of various sounds: the ceaseless click-clack of keyboards typing, phones intermittently ringing, hushed whispers and louder conversations that ebbed and flowed like the tide. All this was suddenly cut through by Sakura's melodious voice, resounding from the intercom. "Good morning, my lovely Whiskers! I have a rather unusual announcement. Everyone, please make your way to the conference room for a mandatory, exciting, and potentially life-saving CPR training!"

A wave of bewilderment, curiosity, and a hint of mirth spread through the office. Colleagues exchanged puzzled glances, their shoulders shrugged in resigned amusement, before they began rising from their desks. We, the employees of Whisker Wonders, were no strangers to unorthodox office activities, but this announcement managed to top even our expectations.

As the crowd of bemused employees filed into the conference room, an unexpected sight greeted us. Standing tall at the front of the room was a literal mountain of a man, or more accurately, a minotaur. His muscular physique stretched the fabric of his tracksuit, which seemed to be crafted out of painted-on latex. The sheer size of this creature was awe-inspiring, his towering form causing the normally high ceiling lights to resemble low-hanging chandeliers. His wide back sported the word "BEAST" in bold, contrasting white letters against the navy-blue track-suit.

"Am I dreaming or did Sakura really just hire a mythical beast-man to teach us CPR?" Hana whispered, her eyes round as saucers and reflecting the disbelief running rampant among us all.

Momo, with her eyebrows hiked up to her hairline, murmured back, "More like a walking, talking mountain."

"Now, now," chimed in Sakura, her grin outshining the sequined dress she was wearing. Her voice hummed with a gleeful undertone as she announced, "Let's not forget our manners. Let's give our very real, and incredibly qualified, CPR instructor a warm Whisker welcome!"

The minotaur, imposing as he was, had a surprising gentleness in his eyes, and a welcoming grin that seemed out of place on his stern, chiseled features. He offered a nod of acknowledgment, which to him, must have felt like a small movement, but looked more akin to a small earthquake to us.

This colossus, whose aura matched his physical stature, held out a gigantic hand in friendly greeting. "Hello everyone, my name's Joe."

At this, a burst of laughter sprang from Hana, breaking the stifling atmosphere that had enveloped the room. She clamped a hand over her mouth, her eyes wide and twinkling with barely suppressed mirth.

"Joe?" She managed to squeak out between snorts of laughter. "I mean, no disrespect, but I was expecting something... more grand, like... Gigantor... or Titanus... or Beefcakeus Maximus." She doubled over at her own joke, struggling to contain her laughter.

The conference room held its breath for a split second, before it filled with roaring laughter. The sheer absurdity of the situation, combined with Hana's infectious laughter, left none immune to the humor of it all. Even our mighty minotaur, Joe, cracked a grin that soon bloomed into a hearty laugh, reverberating around the room like a roll of thunder.

Beside her, Momo and I tried, unsuccessfully, to smother our own laughter. With a poorly veiled smile, I managed to scold her, "Hana, keep it down. We're here to learn, remember?"

"Yeah," Momo agreed, choking back a chuckle, "Remember, this is... a serious session."

In response, Hana simply nodded, the motion looking like a bobblehead doll on a dashboard. Her shoulders shook with laughter as she tried to regain her composure.

Joe, amused at the exchange, nodded in agreement. "Yes, it's a serious session. But a little laughter never hurt anyone." His eyes twinkled with humor, adding to the lighthearted mood of the room. "After all, a happy heart is a healthy heart, right?"

"We're sorry, Mr Joe. Please continue," I added with an amicable smile.

The minotaur returned the nod. "Now, are we ready to learn and have some fun?" He asked, his voice a low rumble of good-natured thunder.

A chorus of affirmatives and nods came from the crowd. Their faces were an eclectic mix of astonishment, intrigue, and amusement. Before us stood Joe, the minotaur, his hands that looked like they could easily cradle a small boulder, dwarfing the mannequin lying lifelessly on the table. "Alright everyone," he began, his deep voice reverberating through the room like a low growl of thunder, "CPR can often be the difference between life and death."

Hana, barely suppressing another round of giggles, whispered to Momo, "Looks like it's a little late for this guy." Momo tried to stifle her giggles behind her hand, making her look like she was trying to hide a mischievous smile behind a fan.

Joe cleared his throat, shooting a playful glare in their direction. "While it's true that our friend here has seen better days, he's a trooper and an excellent learning tool."

He then started to explain the process of CPR, placing his enormous hands on the mannequin's chest. "It's crucial to maintain a steady rhythm when performing chest compressions." He started demonstrating, counting out loud, "One and two and three and ..."

There was a sudden, loud crack. The mannequin's chest had collapsed under the minotaur's strength. Joe, taken aback, looked down at the mannequin, which now looked more like a modern art installation than a CPR training tool. A stunned silence fell over the room, only to be broken by a single snort of laughter.

"I guess he didn't make it, huh?" Hana called out, her laughter spreading contagiously throughout the room.

Joe chuckled sheepishly, rubbing the back of his neck. "Well, it looks like I don't know my own strength. But don't worry!" He bent down, rummaged in a large bag, and triumphantly pulled out another mannequin, albeit one that had seen better days. "Luckily, I always come prepared with spares. Everyone, meet Timmy, our new volunteer."

As Joe gently laid 'Timmy' on the table, I remarked, "Let's hope he's got better luck than the last guy."

With a sheepish grin, Joe resumed the lesson, noticeably gentler with 'Timmy'. However, as the lesson went on, Joe's teaching style evolved into something that resembled more of a comedy act. Each explanation was peppered with misused words and accidental displays of his remarkable strength. A demonstration of the Heimlich maneuver rendered another mannequin useless, and an innocent pat on the back sent a chair skidding across the room.

With each blunder, Joe's reactions grew more comical, his expressions ranging from shock to horror, usually seen in dramatic theatrical plays. We, the employees, were roaring with laughter, our chuckles growing louder with each new disaster. Even our normally stoic HR manager, Aiko, was struggling to suppress her giggles behind her hand.

Finally, as the session came to a close, Joe gathered us around for a final word. His eyes twinkled with amusement as he regarded his audience, who had become more like friends than students.

"Remember, everyone, CPR is about balance. It's about knowing when to be gentle and when to be firm," he paused, a twinkle of humor in his eyes before he added, "And perhaps, for some of us, it's about knowing our own strength."

The room erupted in applause, and Joe took a theatrical bow, his horns nearly scraping the ceiling. Hana perfectly encapsulated our collective sentiment as we left the room, still chuckling: "Well, that was certainly a lesson we'll never forget! Awesome job, Joe!" I looked back at the now battered training dummies and smirked as I shook my head.

CHAPTER 13

When Sakura, our illustrious CEO, called out to me amidst the boisterous cacophony of our office, I felt a chill wind sweep through my insides. "Kazuki," her voice rang clear and pure, like a bell tolling over a hushed sea, "Can you join me in my office, please?" The immediate silence that followed was as thick as a fog, our lively banter evaporating like morning dew in the heat of her attention.

Caught in the crosshairs of this unexpected summons, my heart launched into a frenzied rhythm. I had always been a model employee, meticulously observant of deadlines, respectful of office etiquette, and held cordial relations with my colleagues. A rapid fire carousel of potential slip-ups spun through my mind, but none seemed grave enough to merit a personal audience with Sakura.

My friends and fellow cat girl employees, Hana and Momo, looked just as shell-shocked. Hana's usual spark was dimmed as she whispered, "Oh no..." while Momo, the stoic rock that she is, leaned over to ask, "Did you accidentally forward that inappropriate office meme to everyone, Kazuki?"

Attempting to dispel the building tension, I forced a chuckle and replied, "Maybe she just wants to compliment me on my tie. After all, it is new." The ensuing giggle did little to break the taut silence.

Following in Sakura's wake, I admired the natural grace she commanded. Her long, blonde hair shimmered like a cascade of moonlight against her back. What usually seemed comforting now appeared ominous. The distance to her office, which I'd traversed countless times, felt like an endless gauntlet, every footfall echoing the rhythm of my mounting apprehension.

As we reached her office door, a massive oak monstrosity that suddenly seemed as intimidating as the gates of a fortress, I steeled myself. I'd faced numerous trials and tribulations back on Earth and Silver City, and this was simply another hurdle to leap over.

"Here goes nothing," I muttered to myself, donning a mask of courage. With my heart hammering a chaotic symphony against my ribs, I stepped over the threshold, ready to face whatever awaited me in the lion's den.

A friendly gesture from Sakura beckoned me to the chair that sat across her gigantic desk. Her warm smile was like sunshine breaking through stormy clouds, attempting to bring comfort in an otherwise intimidating setting. I felt my palms turn clammy as I crossed the expansive room, trying to match the pace of my racing heart.

The door swung shut behind me with a thud that sounded like a punctuation mark in the unfolding narrative of my corporate life. The noise reverberated ominously around the room, setting my nerves jangling. Nestling into the plush depths of the chair, I glanced around, my eyes roving over the sophisticated decor. A gallery of Sakura's achievements hung on the walls – framed diplomas, commendations, and pho-

tos of her rubbing shoulders with high-powered elites
– a testament to her esteemed position in the world of
commerce.

Yet, in stark contrast to the high-stakes ambiance,
the office had a welcoming aura. It was a reflection of
Sakura herself – a blend of assertiveness and warmth.
There was a feeling of homeliness among the otherwise austere professional aesthetics. It was disarming
and welcoming, a testament to Sakura's unique lead-
ership style.

Realizing the amount of time I had spent pondering
the decor, I snapped back into the moment. My nerves
were visible; the uncertainty etched on my face was
clear as day. Sakura, noticing this, shot me a reassuring
smile that cut through the tension like a hot knife
through butter.

"You look as if you're about to face a firing squad,
Kazuki," she chided lightly, her voice lilting with
mirth. "Relax, this isn't an inquisition."

At her words, I exhaled, not even realizing that I'd
been holding my breath. The knot of anxiety in my
stomach eased slightly, and I settled back into the

chair, its velvety texture offering an odd sense of comfort.

Sakura began our meeting by casually asking about my experience at Whisker Wonders so far. Her demeanor was more of a friend than a high-profile CEO, a characteristic that was both surprising and comforting. "How have you been finding things here?" She asked.

I thought for a moment before replying, "It's been really fantastic. The team is incredible and supportive, and the environment is... unique, in the best way." My words seemed insignificant compared to the whirlwind of emotions I had experienced during my time at Whisker Wonders, but it was the best I could articulate.

The CEO nodded in response, her eyes glinting with satisfaction. She looked as if she was about to say something when suddenly, her gaze sharpened, her tone turned serious. "Today, Kazuki," she began, "we're here for an evaluation of your work."

My heart plummeted into my stomach at her words. My face must have morphed into an expression of pure panic. Sakura promptly burst into laughter. Her giggles filled the room, echoing off the tall ceilings and melting into the ambient noise of the office beyond the heavy door.

"Oh, Kazuki, your face!" She exclaimed between bouts of laughter, dabbing at the corners of her eyes. "Don't look so horrified. I promise, this isn't as terrifying as you're making it out to be."

A little embarrassed, I cracked a small smile. "You had me scared there for a second, Sakura," I admitted, matching her candidness.

"My goodness," she chuckled, amusement dancing in her eyes. "Well, I apologize. The truth is, Kazuki, you've impressed me."

I blinked, taken aback by her statement. My brain felt as if it had short-circuited. "I... I have?"

"Absolutely," she assured, her gaze as steady as her voice. "You've shown initiative, dedication, and adaptability, qualities I greatly admire. Not only have you excelled in your role as a security specialist, but you've also lent a hand in other departments."

Her following words brought warmth flooding into my cheeks. She mentioned Babs from accounting, how she had spoken highly of me, how I had helped her streamline her processes. Apparently, my contribution had a marked impact on the department's productivity and morale. I had been oblivious to the degree of my influence; hearing it from the CEO herself left me astonished.

"That's... That's good to hear," I stammered, my mind still trying to comprehend her words. "I'm just trying to do my part, I guess."

Sakura laughed again, her cheer filling the room. "And you're doing it brilliantly, Kazuki. I just wanted to acknowledge that."

Her words settled within me, igniting a warmth in my chest. I managed to stutter out my thanks, still overwhelmed by the praise. Sakura waved off my gratitude, her smile never leaving her face.

"And that, Kazuki, is how we do things at Whisker Wonders. We believe in acknowledging good work, promoting a healthy work environment and... of course, a bit of fun," Sakura finished with a grin, an impish sparkle in her eyes.

She leaned back in her chair, her eye sparkling in the soft light from the windows. Her gaze was sharp, but her smile softened the intensity, turning it into a fond, appreciative expression.

My heart swelled, a mix of relief and pride coursing through me. A chuckle escaped my lips as the reality sunk in. "A 'bit' of fun is an understatement, I think," I quipped, recalling the recent CPR training with our 'minotaur' instructor. The memory brought a fresh wave of laughter, and even Sakura chuckled along.

The tension in the room evaporated, replaced by a warm camaraderie. Our laughter echoed off the walls, adding a human touch to the otherwise imposing office. As our laughter subsided, I finally felt at ease, realizing that this 'intimidating' meeting was nothing more than a casual conversation laced with positive feedback and friendly banter.

"There's one more thing, Kazuki," Sakura said, her voice returning to a more serious tone. I looked at her, my nerves instantly making a comeback. She seemed to sense this, her face splitting into a grin. "Don't look so terrified again! It's good news."

My heart, which had jumped into my throat, slowly sank back to its rightful place. I let out a sigh, shaking my head in exasperation. "You really enjoy scaring me, don't you?"

She laughed, a hearty sound that bounced around the room. "Just a little," she admitted with a mischievous wink. "Now, let's get back to the good news. Given the growth we've seen from you over the past few month I want to..."

My jaw dropped in surprise. Was I hearing this right? "Wait...are you...?" I stuttered, unable to finish the sentence.

"Promoting you?" she supplied a smile playing on her lips. "Yes, I am. You've proven yourself to be an asset to Whisker Wonders, and I believe you should be rewarded. Your new title is Business Analyst. You're still in charge of security but I think Security Specialist Business Analyst is a mouthful."

I smirked. "Just a bit."

A wave of disbelief washed over me. This was beyond anything I had expected when I walked into this room. "I...I don't know what to say, Sakura. I'm... thank you. This is incredible." My voice was barely a whisper, the words choked by the overwhelming emotions I was feeling.

Her laughter echoed in the room once more, this time sounding triumphant. "You're very welcome, Kazuki. You've earned it. You will receive a 25% raise, company card, and laptop when you need to work from home. Aiko and I are working on a job description but we'll iron all that out later."

As I left Sakura's office that day, my head was spinning with the whirlwind of emotions I had experienced. It was a day of surprises, laughter, and life-changing news. The prospect of a new challenge was thrilling, but for now, I was still soaking in the pleasant shock of the unexpected promotion. A glance toward the battered mannequin 'Timmy' in the trash can in the conference room, made me chuckle, reminding me of the unconventional yet fulfilling world I had stepped into. Whisker Wonders indeed had a flair for the dramatic, but it was a drama I was more than willing to be a part of.

CHAPTER 14

"A promotion? Holy crap!" Hana's words bounced off the office walls, drawing the attention of every nearby employee. Her eyes as wide as saucers and the grin on her face stretching from ear to ear. With each spring in her step, it looked as if she was getting ready to launch into orbit any second now.

Momo chimed in, her voice a soothing balm of sanity amidst Hana's infectious excitement. "Our very own Kazuki, scaling the corporate ladder like a seasoned climber. Is there anything you can't do?" Her words were soaked in pride, and her dark eyes sparkled warmly as she extended her hand in a professional congratulatory shake followed with a flirtatious wink.

I shook her hand, feeling the enormity of the moment pressing down on me. "Honestly, guys," I said, a soft chuckle escaping my lips, "I'm just trying not to trip over my own feet in this whirlwind of a place. I'm as shocked as anyone about this promotion."

Momo's eyes suddenly lit up, her gaze flicking to Hana and then back to me, a clear sign of a brainwave. "I've got it," she declared, her voice ringing with certainty.

Casting a wary glance at Momo's gleeful expression, I replied, "Alright, what's this master plan?"

Momo's grin widened. "A celebration, of course! A man can't get a promotion and not celebrate. It's practically illegal!" She cast a side glance at Hana, who was practically bouncing on her toes at this point, her nod vigorous.

"And just how are we celebrating?" I asked, curiosity piqued by their theatrics.

"Well," Momo said, her voice dropping into a dramatic whisper, "there's this new sushi place that just opened down the street. The 'Whelp!'reviews are great, and they've got this mega monster roll that I've been dying to try."

"Celebrating with sushi? Sounds like a plan. I'm in."

******

We approached Silver City Sushi Bar, its polished sign gleaming beneath the city's radiant lights. The sign hanging over the entrance twinkled with the reflection of the Silver City skyline. Set against the backdrop of the city's incessant vibrancy, the sushi bar was a beacon of intrigue, its architectural design an appealing blend of tradition and modernity.

The façade of the sushi bar was a visual delight, an amalgamation of sleek modernistic design and the timeless aesthetic of Silver City's own architecture. Glass panels intersected with metal accents, reflecting the city's characteristic steel structures, while the display window invited passersby to gaze upon an indoor oasis, a tranquil tableau of Silver City greenery.

As I pulled open the restaurant's glass door, a rush of warm, enticing air greeted us. Inside, Silver City Sushi Bar was a sensory haven. Soft light from hanging lanterns painted the interiors with an inviting glow, illuminating the exquisite details around. The sushi bar occupied a prime spot in the room, chefs moving behind it with a fluid grace, their meticulous hands crafting edible works of art.

One side of the restaurant boasted a collection of sake bottles, a nod to brewing traditions from around the world. In contrast, the opposite side featured an array of semi-private booths, their seclusion emphasized by intricately designed sliding doors, the blend of Silver City and far-eastern artwork hinting at the cultural fusion this place embodied.

The dark wood flooring shone under the lanterns' soft light, reflecting the inviting ambiance. The air was a tapestry of tantalizing aromas – the tang of rice vinegar, the briny freshness of seaweed, and the subtle, spicy notes of wasabi and pickled ginger.

Silver City Sushi Bar was not just another restaurant; it was an immersion into a world where Silver City's contemporary charm met traditional culinary artistry. This wasn't just about the sushi; it was an exploration of culinary culture nestled in the heart of Silver City. As I took in the scene, a grin of anticipation played on my lips. This was definitely a fitting place for a celebration.

Our party of three was guided to a cozy nook in the restaurant's far corner, offering a modicum of privacy that seemed perfect for our celebratory feast. The location was choice, positioned snugly against an expanse of wall showcasing a breathtaking mural. It was an artful tableau of stars caught mid-twirl in a cosmic dance, a vivid reminder of the city from which our beloved sushi bar took its name.

The booth was stylish and cozy; the seats were a deep-cushioned sanctuary promising comfort, while the polished table, crafted from dark, almost ebony, wood, added a touch of sophistication. It was as though we had slipped into another world - one where comfort and elegance were no longer at odds.

As I sank into the plush upholstery, the seat seemed to embrace me like an old friend. Across the table, Hana and Momo, buoyant with excitement, slid into their own seats. The table between us, polished to a near mirror finish, gleamed in the gentle glow cascading from a decorative lantern overhead.

Our menus were passed to us by the hostess, each one a work of art in its own right. Leather-bound and embossed with the ornate emblem of Silver City

Sushi Bar, they felt more like antique books than mere listings of food. As we cracked them open, we were met with an array of sushi options, each bearing a name that sounded more like an exotic adventure than a meal.

Breaking our silence, Hana excitedly jabbed her finger at an item on her menu. "Guys, check this out!" she exclaimed. Her eyes sparkled with excitement as she read, "'Stellar Spiral', composed of juicy starfruit and succulent lunar crab. How amazing does that sound?"

"Perfectly fitting for Silver City, I'd say," Momo responded, a playful chuckle escaping her lips. She swept her fingers down her own menu, stopping on a roll that had caught her interest. "Now listen to this one. It's called the 'Galaxy Glider', packed with what they claim to be Venusian eel and a sauce created from fiery solar peppers. Now that's a gastronomic expedition if I've ever heard of one!"

"Sounds like a gastrointestinal explosion on the toilet too," Hana joked.

The laughter that followed was easy and filled the air around us with warmth. Even though the day had started with a nerve-wracking surprise, the evening was shaping into something memorable, thanks to the company of friends and a menu full of potential culinary adventures.

My eyes darted over the menu, finally landing on a roll that seemed too tempting to resist. The 'Comet Crunch', a tantalizing blend of meteor shrimp and asteroid avocados, both named to maintain the restaurant's otherworldly theme.

Just as the conversation was hitting a comedic peak, a soft tinkling sound cut through our laughter. The source was a figure delicately weaving her way through the restaurant. A graceful kitsune waitress, as bewitching as the moon's allure, was heading our way. She moved with the elegance of a koi swimming upstream, the fan of her multiple tails streaming behind her like shimmering silk ribbons. Her golden fur caught the soft light of the overhead lanterns, glowing with an ethereal luminescence, while her captivating eyes sparkled with an enticing charm that was hard to ignore.

Gently sliding into our sphere of conversation, her voice, as soft as the notes of a koto, floated toward us, "Good evening, I'm Kira. I'll be your server tonight.

Have you decided on your orders?" Her question seemed loaded with an implicit invitation, her eyes almost audibly twinkling as they met mine. I could feel my face heating up a bit under her gaze.

Oblivious to the subtle electricity in the air, I scanned my menu one last time before locking in my choices. "I'd like the Comet Crunch roll, please, and… uh," I paused, considering the array of unusual drinks on offer, "I think I'll go with a Nebula Nectar for my drink."

Momo jumped in next, her eyes alight with barely suppressed mischief. "The Galaxy Glider roll for me," she declared, her eyes glinting with concealed amusement as she added, "And to wash that down, I'll take an Orion's Onyx, please."

Hana, ever the adventurous eater, decided to order something that even I hadn't dared to try. "I'll have the Stellar Spiral roll," she chimed in enthusiastically, "and to accompany it, a Cosmic Cosmo."

Kira jotted down our orders with the deftness of a practiced scribe, her fluffy tails swaying gently with each stroke of her pen. As she collected our menus, she gifted me another of her captivating glances. Then, with a swish of her tails that seemed choreographed to bewitch, she floated away from our table, leaving in her wake an atmosphere tinged with a peculiarly charming vibe.

No sooner had she left than Hana erupted into a fit of giggles, her laughter bouncing off the booth's walls. "Kazuki," she gasped between giggles, poking me with her elbow, "Are you really that blind? Kira was eyeballing you like a hot fudge sundae!"

Joining the teasing, Momo roared with laughter, her mischievous tone bubbling over like an uncorked bottle of champagne. "She was practically undressing you with her eyes, Kazuki!" She chimed in, her words accompanied by an exaggerated mimicry of Kira's infatuated gaze.

Heat rushed up my neck and into my cheeks. "What? Really?" I stuttered, my pulse inexplicably speeding up at their revelation. A thrill shot through me, and suddenly, I found my fingers nervously fidgeting with the napkin in my lap, my lips involuntarily curving into a bashful smile.

It felt like time turned into a lazy cat, leisurely stretching itself out, as we found ourselves enveloped in the ambience of the restaurant. Laughter bubbled in the air around us, a contagion more potent than any cosmic phenomenon. Before we knew it, half an hour breezed by, as elusive as a shooting star, and Kira made her grand re-entry. Balancing an array of culinary delights and an assortment of radiant drinks, she resembled a celestial goddess gracing us with gifts from the heavens.

Among the culinary parade, the first to command my attention was the Comet Crunch roll. It was a spectacle that could easily rival a supernova's brilliance. The topaz-toned fish, like slices of a fallen star, were arranged with an artistic precision atop mounds of pearly, fragrant rice. Sprinkled with a generous dash of glittering 'comet dust,' the roll seemed to encapsulate the entire cosmos in its inviting form. The crunch against my teeth gave way to a deluge of taste that left me momentarily starstruck. "Wow...this is...wow," I stuttered, the explosion of flavors rendering me momentarily inarticulate.

Beside me, Momo was served her Galaxy Glider roll, which looked like it had been plucked straight out of a colorful painting. The striking contrast of the deep violet hued fish, garnished with shimmering edible gold flakes, made it a feast for the eyes before it even became one for the palate. Momo sank her teeth into it and let out a sound akin to a supernova's birth. "By the seven stars, this is a culinary miracle!" she exclaimed, her eyes twinkling like twin galaxies.

Across from us, Hana's face lit up at the sight of her Stellar Spiral roll, a spiraling tower that was an interstellar journey in itself. Each layer was constructed with meticulous care, forming a mosaic of enticing colors. She dived into her meal, and the ensuing look of pure ecstasy on her face would have made celestial deities green with envy. "This...this is like dining in heaven or somewhere like heaven if there isn't a heaven!" She declared, shaking her head in sheer disbelief.

The drinks, as expected, had their own astral magic to them. My Nebula Nectar was a mesmerizing swirl of pastel hues, a taste that I can only describe as what I'd imagine stardust would taste like if mixed with the most succulent fruits from across the universe, and a fizz that was akin to sipping a celestial champagne. Momo's Orion's Onyx was a paradox - as dark as a starless night yet as sweet as summer berries from a sun-kissed planet, a tangy twist that surprised and delighted the senses. Hana's Cosmic Cosmo lived up to its vibrant violet reputation, causing Hana to theatrically announce, "I feel like I'm drinking the dreams of a star!"

"Whatever the hell that means," I replied with a raised brow.

"Kazuki," Momo playfully jabbed, "I'm pretty sure Kira was eyeing you the same way we were eyeing our sushi rolls."

Chiming in on the joke, Hana added, "Maybe Kira wants a taste of your Nebula Nectar, Kazuki!" Her playful wink was enough to fuel another bout of uproarious laughter.

I leaned back in my seat and put my hands behind my head and smirked. "Well, I've got plenty of nectar to go around."

CHAPTER 15

Over the next week, my job at Whisker Wonders, while not drastically different post-promotion, was imbued with a new sense of purpose. I am a Business Analyst now. The title felt like a shiny new badge pinned proudly to my chest.

Sakura had hinted at additional responsibilities coming my way, but those were as yet undefined, vague as a whisper on the wind. She promised to work out the kinks and, in truth, I was intrigued by the unknown that lay ahead. Sakura had shown faith in me by bestowing this promotion and I had complete trust that she'd lead me down the right path.

In the midst of this exciting uncertainty, one change presented itself with palpable reality – my new business cards. Odd as it may sound, I awaited their arrival with the anticipation of a child before Christmas. When they were finally delivered, holding that card in my hands was akin to gripping a firm handshake of recognition. There it was, my name and the words 'Business Analyst" in dark bold print.

Reflecting on the journey that had led me to this moment, I felt a surge of gratification. The countless hours spent fortifying Whisker Wonders' security systems, the bonds formed with my team, the trials, the triumphs - they all culminated in this tangible acknowledgment of my worth. The business card was more than just a rectangle of cardboard. It was a testament to my growth, a physical testament of my merit, and holding it made me swell with a sense of accomplishment.

One might say that my life at Whisker Wonders, post-promotion, had become the quintessence of professionalism, a series of strictly regimented tasks and responsibilities that came with my new job title. But that would be an assumption founded on a gross misunderstanding of the kind of mischief my colleagues, especially one feline in particular, were prone to. Enter Hana, the enigmatic cat girl with her lustrous chestnut hair, always seemingly caught in a non-existent wind. Her embodiment of mischief was akin playful and unpredictable, capable of upending the calmest of days.

Hana sauntered up to my desk, her tail twitching in a rhythm that spelled playful devilry. An impish glint sparkled in her emerald-green eyes as she daintily slid a sealed envelope toward me. The sheen of her glossy pink lips curled into a smirk, her flawless face radiant under the soft glow of the overhead lights.

"What's this?" I queried, my brow arching involuntarily in suspicion as I scrutinized the envelope. The seemingly innocent package was enough to ignite a conflagration of curiosity within me.

A provocative chuckle slipped from her lips as she replied, "A little something for you to...work on later." Her voice, warm and as tantalizing as a forbidden secret, emphasized 'work on,' enticing me further into her scheme. Without another word, she performed a swift pirouette, her form a symphony of grace, and retreated to her desk, leaving me intrigued and in the throes of a bewildering fascination.

Holding back a laugh at her antics, I gently unsealed the envelope. My fingers, already sensing the mischief that lay within, trembled slightly. As I withdrew the contents, my world came to a grinding halt. I found myself holding a photocopy - but this was no ordinary piece of stationary. This was a photocopy of Hana's bare chest. A loud, shocked, "Wow!" ricocheted out of my mouth, tearing through the tranquility of the office. As the echo of my outburst faded, heads turned, curious eyes wondering what could have caused my sudden commotion.

Just then, amidst the sea of surprise that had engulfed me, my phone buzzed impatiently, snapping me back to reality. A text from Hana lit up the screen, "Well, do you like it? It's a very important task for you to take charge of." My face instantly matched the color of a ripened cherry as I hurriedly replaced the risque photocopy back into the envelope, quickly concealing it within the safe confines of my suit blazer's inner pocket.

Still reeling, I managed to punch a reply into my phone, "You're crazy. How on earth did you manage to do that without getting caught?" The question was valid, considering our office was a hive of activity, never deserted.

Her reply was swift and unabashed, "I'm very sneaky!" Shaking my head, a grin tugged at my lips. This was life at Whisker Wonders; unpredictable, humorous, and just a tad bit crazy, particularly with Hana in the mix. And as for the task at hand, well, that was a matter for later.

******

Post lunchtime, Momo, with her radiant green hair glinting under the fluorescent office lights, made her way toward my cubicle. Her walk was not just a walk, but a deliberate, teasing saunter that had heads turning and eyes following her across the room. She possessed a playful glint in her eyes and a mischievous smirk playing on her lips.

She leaned against my cubicle divider, her casual poise and confident aura transforming our everyday office into a scene straight out of an anime. She outstretched her hand, presenting me with a tightly sealed envelope, its mysterious contents an open secret between the two of us.

"Special delivery for Mr. Kazuki," she purred, winking at me. I could feel the blood rushing to my cheeks, turning them a shade similar to cherry blossoms. I was certain of the envelope's contents. After all, not long before, Hana had boldly gifted me a photocopy of her bare chest, encased in the anonymity of a similar envelope.

With Momo's echoing laughter as my only company, I gingerly accepted the envelope, my hand brushing against hers in the exchange. She turned on her heel, her laughter trailing behind her as she sashayed back to her desk. Her captivating green eyes watched me with anticipation.

Trepidation mixing with curiosity, I carefully broke the seal, slowly revealing the image within. It wasn't Hana's daring prank repeating itself, but something different, something unexpected. The envelope held a photocopy of Momo's bare backside. A look of absolute shock washed over my face.Choking on my coffee, I sprayed a mouthful across my keyboard, the dark liquid splattering across the keys like abstract art.

Momo's laughter from her cubicle echoed around the room, punctuating the absurdity of the moment.

Still reeling from the shock, I grasped at my smartphone, its cool, familiar surface grounding me in the realm of normalcy. I hastily pulled up a group chat with Momo and Hana. My fingers flew across the screen, furiously typing a mix of disbelief and humor. "You two are completely off your rockers," I texted, a slight chuckle escaping me despite the chaos. "The 'gifts' you've bestowed are... appreciated, but they're pushing the envelope - quite literally. You're skating on thin ice here, risking our professional lives with your cheeky stunts."

As the message sent, I leaned back in my chair, casting a wary glance toward Momo's desk. The corners of her mouth twitched upward, revealing a cat-like grin that screamed 'mission accomplished.' My phone vibrated, pulling my attention back to the glowing screen.

Momo was first to respond. "Too smart to get caught," her message read, a digital testament to the sly confidence she wore like a second skin. I could practically hear the prideful lilt in her voice, assuring me she had everything under control.

A moment later, a new text from Hana popped onto the screen. "You know," she wrote, her digital tone deceptively casual, "Babs has been swooning over you for quite some time. Maybe she should be the next to... contribute? I bet she'd make quite the impression. She should send a copy of her snatch!"

Before I had the chance to digest Hana's impish proposal, another message buzzed in, this one from Momo again. "And we absolutely can't leave out Rebecca. She should definitely join in on the fun. The only question is, what should she 'copy'?"

The mental image of my AI assistant Rebecca trying to participate in this prank triggered an unexpected burst of laughter. As I was about to reply, I noticed a stern figure navigating the office landscape from the corner of my eye. It was Aiko, our in-house law enforcer and HR manager. Her brown hair was tied in a strict bun, matching the cold expression on her face. The rim of her glasses caught the office light, giving her an almost predatory look as she made her rounds. She needed to smile more because she was a very attractive cat girl.

My fingers danced across the screen, sending a swift warning to my fearless pranksters. "Alert, ladies! Aiko's on her routine patrol. You'd better transform into perfect employees unless you want a one-way trip to her office."

With the message sent, I sat back, the soft glow of the smartphone screen illuminating the office twilight. The scene froze there once again, poised for the next unpredictable development in our slice-of-life comedy.

CHAPTER 16

One particular evening, after bidding goodbye to my cat girl co-workers at the office, I found myself making a beeline to the Silver City Strikers dojo, my second home of sorts, well other than Momo and Hana's apartment. Chozen, my close drow friend and the dojo's revered sensei, had somehow managed to rope me into a part-time teaching gig. His convincing charm was hard to refuse. Initially, I was apprehensive. I was there for my own training, a quiet observer and practitioner of martial arts. But Chozen saw something else—a potential instructor. Despite my reservations, I decided to take the plunge and agreed to teach a group of five students the basics of

Wing Chun Kung Fu. The dojo was focused on karate and I wasn't sure kung fu would mix well with what they were being taught. Chozen assured me that it wouldn't be a problem. Five of his most promising students were interested in dipping their toe in Wing Chun style Kung Fu. I was excited and apprehensive. I knew I had master level skills in the martial art, but I was not blessed with master level teaching skills. It was nice to be called sensei though, I'm not going to lie.

The first among my new wards was Theo, a young man carrying the grace of his half-elf lineage. His lanky silhouette was well-toned, and a mop of auburn hair often fell over his sharp, earnest eyes. "Wing Chun is all about balance, right?" He asked during our first session, his enthusiasm bubbling over like a fresh cup of coffee. I had chuckled at his energetic eagerness, reminding him that it was also about patience.

Then, along came Ragnor, a sturdy wall of a man, dwarf heritage evident in his build. His fiery red hair and beard often bristled when he got the stance wrong, his frustration almost tangible. "This is harder than forging iron," he once grumbled during a particularly grueling session. I laughed, assuring him that he'd soon be as fluid as water, just as Wing Chun demanded. His small stature did prove to make things a little more difficult.

The third addition to my motley crew was Maris, a graceful woman with silver hair, carrying the fluidity of her sylph roots. Her movements were akin to a leaf carried by the wind, effortless and rhythmic. She was a dancer trying to fit into the disciplined framework of Wing Chun. "This isn't a waltz, Maris," I had reminded her during an exercise, her laughter filling the dojo as she attempted the drill again.

Zephyr, the fourth student, had the distinctive characteristics of a tiefling. His indigo skin and intense gold eyes were striking, but it was his agility and focus that marked him as an exceptional student. He once declared, "I've mastered the poker face," during a particularly intense sparring session, sending the entire class into a round of chuckles.

Last, but never least, was Caelia. The petite woman had halfling roots, which were evident in her diminutive stature. Her curly brown hair and twinkling hazel eyes shone with a determination that was ten times her size. "I'll grow a few more inches before next class to make things easier," she joked, her quip breaking the tension during a tough lesson.

There they were, my group of five—a delightful blend of personalities and backgrounds. Each one was unique, like different notes forming a harmonious melody, their respective strengths and traits adding color to the canvas of Wing Chun.

A couple of weeks into teaching, Momo, my green-haired hottie cat girlfriend companion decided to drop by one evening. She perched herself at the back of the dojo, her green hair a vivid contrast against the wooden walls. Her presence added a different kind of energy, making the entire experience even more vibrant.

"Alright, people," I called out, clapping my hands together. Their voices fell into a hush as they aligned themselves in a row, a line-up of diverse, eager faces.

"Tonight," I began, holding my arms out, palms open, "we delve into the heart of Wing Chun—Chi Sao or 'sticky hands.'" There were nods of under-standing, glimmers of anticipation mirrored in their eyes. I walked them through the stance, eyes moving across the room to ensure the 'Bong Sao' was just right—elbows tucked in, arms extended, and palms wide open.

Pairing them off was the next step. I pitted Theo with Zephyr, their youthful vibrancy an ideal match. Maris was with Ragnor—a graceful sylph dancing against a robust dwarf, and I decided to accompany Caelia. The room filled with an electric energy as they fell into their stances.

I offered a reminder, my gaze fixating on Ragnor. "Remember, Wing Chun isn't about the brawn, it's about balance, about harmony. Keep your muscles relaxed." He blinked, looking down at his beefy arms before offering a comically bashful grin. Laughter trickled through the room, a shared mirth that weaved us closer.

The rhythmic slap of palms meeting, a ballet of hands and bodies, echoed throughout the room. Theo and Zephyr, while a symphony of youthful energy, sometimes forgot the flow. "Theo, don't let your stiffness break the rhythm. It's a dance, remember?" His nod, accompanied by a sheepish smile, signaled understanding.

Caelia was a wonder. Her small form moved fluidly, a testament to her will and agility. When she succeeded in landing a soft punch on my shoulder, her face lit up with unfiltered joy. "Ha! That fertilizer I put on myself to grow taller strategy worked," she exclaimed, her comment sending waves of laughter across the dojo. We all shared in her victory, a silent testament to our growing bond.

On the other side of the dojo, Maris and Ragnor were a study in contrast. Maris, her flexibility evident in her graceful maneuvers, faced off against Ragnor's vigorous dwarf strength. The combination was unexpectedly harmonious. "It's like waltzing with a bear, Kazuki!" Maris shouted across the room, and Ragnor's boisterous laughter echoed in response.

As our training approached its end, I found myself amidst the radiating energy of five exuberant students, each glistening with sweat but smiling broadly. Each laughter, every shared triumph, even the grueling practices.

I concluded the lesson, my words echoing in the dojo, "Persistence and practice are the keys to mastering Chi Sao. We strive for progress, not perfection."

Their fervent nods spoke of an understanding deeper than words.

******

In the hushed aftermath of the departed students, the dojo was a serene, private world of its own. The echo of laughter and earnest shouts of dedication had been replaced with the soft hum of silence. As I locked the doors, shutting away the world outside, the sole sound was the soft click of the lock, a seal on the day's hard work.

The echo of Momo's voice bounced across the room, shattering the quietude. "Kazuki," she began, her words heavy with an earnest sincerity, "you were seriously impressive tonight." Her words swirled around me, landing like a soft feather upon my heart.

I turned to her, finding her splayed on one of the wooden benches, her vivid green hair splayed out like a vibrant halo. The fluorescent lights caught in her emerald eyes, making them gleam with an unspoken admiration. "Something about seeing you take charge...It's very...attractive," she confessed, her voice barely above a whisper.

Her candid compliment caught me off-guard, triggering a flush that spread warmth across my face. Grinning, I retorted, "Is that so?" My voice dipped into a playful tone, my heart fluttering with the fresh surge of exhilaration.

With a confident nod, she added, "How about you give me a quick lesson? Just for me?" Her words lingered in the air, laden with anticipation. Her challenge, wrapped within a coy request, was too tempting to refuse.

"Fair warning, Momo," I cautioned, my index finger wagging in the air between us, "I won't go easy on you." Her determination flared bright in her eyes, and she responded with a resolute nod.

Our impromptu lesson began with the stance. Momo's first attempts were clumsy and stiff, but she didn't falter. Instead, every stumble was met with giggles, every fall an excuse to wrap her arms around me for support. Our martial arts lesson quickly turned into a dance of jest and flirtation, our giggles resonating within the confines of the dojo.

"Your hand goes here, Momo," I'd instruct, guiding her into the correct stance, our bodies closer than necessary. Her giggles tickled my ears, our shared warmth a comforting balm against the chill of the night.

Despite her struggles, Momo's spirit didn't dampen. "This is way harder than it looks," she grumbled, puffing out her cheeks in a display of mock frustration. Yet, her eyes sparkled with a determination that spoke volumes.

"And that, Momo," I said, brushing a loose strand of hair away from her face, "is the beauty and challenge of martial arts." Our eyes met, the electric connection between us was strong even in the dim dojo.

Our kung fu lesson was a failure in traditional terms, but as a vehicle for laughter and shared memories, it was a grand success. The dojo became our playground, our laughter the only score we cared for.

Momo's slender fingers curled around the nape of my neck, pulling me closer. Her emerald eyes sparkled with a playful glint as our faces moved nearer. The soft scent of her shampoo wafted through the air, filling my senses with a comforting familiarity. Her lips found mine, capturing me in a warm, gentle kiss. They tasted of sweet strawberries and a hint of mischief, a combination as enchanting as the girl herself.

As she pulled away, leaving me slightly breathless, she wore a triumphant grin. Her eyebrows bounced upward suggestively, the mischievous glint in her eyes now even brighter. "Why don't I give you a lesson now?" She proposed, her voice honeyed and rich with implied promise.

A chuckle rumbled in my chest at her statement. Momo, always ready to turn the tables. I blinked at her, a playful smile pulling at my lips. "And what kind of lesson would that be?" I asked, my heart thudding expectantly in my chest.

Momo's mischievousness reached new heights as her slender fingers slid under the waistband of my athletic pants. Her touch sent an unexpected jolt of electricity racing through me. "How does that feel?" She inquired, her voice barely a whisper yet carrying a weight of anticipation.

A wave of warmth washed over me. "It feels pretty good," I admitted, the corners of my mouth twitching into a playful smirk. "But it would feel even better if we weren't standing directly in front of a window." I let out a snort of laughter at the absurdity of our situation.

Momo's brow cocked upward at my comment, her playful demeanor unfazed. "You don't want people to watch us?" she quipped back, her tone equal parts jest and curiosity.

I chuckled at her retort. "It's not that," I began, my gaze drifting toward the dojo's entrance, "I just don't want passersby getting the wrong impression about what we're teaching in here. I'm pretty sure Chozen wouldn't appreciate this kind of advertising."

She shrugged in response, a twinkle in her eyes. "Suit yourself, Kazuki. We can go wherever you like."

A quick scan of the dojo led my eyes to one of the offices. Within it, a large, comfortable sofa beckoned. The perfect spot. "How about here?" I suggested, leading her into the room.

Momo's eyes roved over the couch before she nodded. "This will work," she confirmed. Without missing a beat, she deftly pulled her tight shirt over her head. The sudden reveal left me momentarily stunned. My eyes widened as I took in her sheer beauty.

Momo was, without a doubt, a masterpiece of the gods. Her every feature was a testament to their divine craftsmanship. Standing there, in the warm glow of the office lights, she was an ethereal beauty, the perfect blend of strength and allure.

With a matching grin, I returned the favor, pulling off my own shirt. Momo's eyes widened, her gaze tracing the contours of my muscular chest, as she let out an appreciative gasp. Her hands gently made their way to my abs, each touch feeling like a lightning bolt straight to my heart.

Taking the game a step further, I slipped my hand into the front of her form-fitting yoga pants. The sudden movement caused her to gasp, her body shuddering against mine. My fingers delved into the warm wetness, exploring her gently. The reaction was immediate and instinctive. "You're excited. I can tell." I whispered into her ear, my voice a low husk.

Her response was a sharp intake of breath. Her lower lip found its way between her teeth, her eyes closing as she surrendered herself to the sensation. "You have no idea," she breathed, her voice shaky with arousal. "That feels so good."

In one seamless, sinuous motion, Momo shimmied out of her yoga pants and underwear. The fabric pooled around her ankles like molten silver, revealing the flawless expanse of her hips and luscious thighs. My heart pounded in my chest like a tribal drum, each thump echoing her mesmerizing rhythm.

I found my hands unconsciously moving to appreciate the feminine artwork before me. My palms cupped her buttocks, relishing the perfect paradox they presented - soft as a downy feather yet firm, testimony to her dedicated fitness routine. They were the ultimate combination, just like the woman who owned them.

Our gazes locked, a silent conversation flowing between us. A flicker of challenge ignited in her emerald eyes, stroking my competitive spirit. Suddenly, I found myself lifting her effortlessly. The surprised yelp she let out mixed with our shared laughter, the sound echoing around the room and adding a unique note to our intimate symphony.

With a playful wink, I tossed her onto the expansive sofa. The plush cushions enveloped her figure as she landed, her vibrant green eyes wide with surprise and intrigue. "Kazuki!" She protested, though the laughter bubbling from her lips contradicted her feigned shock.

I shrugged, a devilish grin tugging at my lips. "What? I thought you liked surprises."

Her playful swat missed as I dodged, her feigned glare melting into an appreciative grin. "You certainly know how to keep things interesting," she conceded. Her admission only served to amplify the spark in her eyes. I could tell that my 'take charge' display had stirred something within her. The thrill of the chase, the unpredictability, the raw desire - it all added up to a scenario neither of us had anticipated happening tonight at the dojo but were more than willing to explore.

With a swift motion that was more reflex than thought, I kicked off my pants, letting them join the discarded pile of our clothes on the floor. There was a rush of cool air against my heated skin, a fleeting sensation that was immediately replaced by the searing warmth of Momo's body. Our bare skin met, the collision sending a tsunami of lust coursing through my veins.

As I gently positioned myself on top of her, it felt as though two magnetic forces were coming together - our bodies finding their way back to each other naturally, seamlessly. A heady sigh escaped her as our bodies pressed closer, her contours fitting perfectly against mine.

Our lips met in a fervent exchange, each kiss stroking the raging fire of our desire. Her lips were a blend of sweetness and warmth, an intoxicating mixture that left me drunk on her essence. With every taste, every shared breath, I found myself spiraling deeper into the whirlpool of our shared passion.

Her fingers traced paths of fire across my back, each touch light, yet full of a desperation that mirrored my own. Her body writhed underneath mine, a silent entreaty that sent a jolt of desire through my already trembling body.

As her breathy voice whispered my name, a rush of anticipation ran down my spine. "Kazuki," she purred in my ear, her voice no more than a soft whimper, "I need you...now."

The whispered words shattered the last remaining shards of my self-control. I was not just Kazuki, the man who taught kung fu, or the business analyst at Whisker Wonders. In that moment, I was a man ablaze with raw desire, captured entirely by the enchanting nymph beneath me.

The primal growl that left my throat resonated in the room, reverberating off the walls before drowning in the sea of passion enveloping us. Eager to satisfy her command, I surrendered to the wild rhythm of our heartbeats, preparing to navigate the turbulent seas of passion we had only just begun to charter.

Slowly, with the precision of a seasoned lover mindful of the sacred dance, I found myself enveloped in the warmth of her being. Each slow thrust sent waves of pleasure radiating out from where our bodies met, and Momo, under my gentle exploration, gasped, a soft, melodious sound. It was as if we had uncovered a secret language, and every gasp, every shudder was a word in a discourse of pleasure. The sensation, so intense, was akin to a lightning bolt, scattering a shower of sparks that touched every nerve, setting her body alight.

Yet, in the midst of this torrent of feelings, I maintained a tender rhythm. Each movement was gentle, deliberate, echoing the rhythmic sway of a slow dance under a moonlit sky. My self-control was like a melody composed of softer notes, setting the stage for the grand symphony to follow.

However, as the seconds blurred into minutes, the tempo of our dance changed. The raging inferno within me began to dictate the rhythm. The slow and tender movements evolved into a passionate dance, our bodies locked in an intimate waltz that spoke volumes of our shared desire. We moved in unison, our bodies instinctively finding their rhythm, a testament to the unspoken connection between us. Each thrust was a fervent affirmation, a testament to the consuming passion that had us in its fiery grip.

The quiet of the room was punctuated by Momo's moans, the sweetest melody that played over the symphony of our beating hearts. Every gasp, every whimper was a harmony in our song of shared pleasure, a testament to the ecstasy that rippled through her.

As the tempo escalated, the room was filled with the sound of Momo's voice, the intensity of her pleasure resonating in her cries. Each syllable of my name that she breathed out between gasps became my beacon, guiding me through the stormy sea of desire. The sound of her voice, laced with ecstasy, was more potent than any aphrodisiac, driving me further into the abyss of pleasure.

Suddenly, her body arched off the sofa, a silent scream frozen on her lips as the wave of pleasure crashed over her. Her muscles contracted around me in an intimate grip, her body convulsing under the sheer intensity of her climax. Her channel grabbed my cock like a vice bringing me to a violent crescendo. I filled her with my precious seed. As the whirlwind of sensations began to calm, I took a moment to appreciate the scene. Momo, my sassy green-eyed enchantress, lay beneath me, her skin glowing under the dim office lights.

CHAPTER 17

It was one of those days at Whisker Wonders where time seemed to drag on forever. The persistent tap-tap-tap of my fingers on the keyboard echoed in the otherwise silent room. Sakura had dumped a formidable stack of new projects on my desk earlier, and I was buried deep within their intricacies, working to unlock potential efficiencies. The office's fluorescent lights overhead gave everything a surreal glow, contrasting with the soft drizzling rain outside. The droplets played a rhythmic dance against the windows, and I occasionally caught myself losing focus, entranced by their mesmerizing patterns.

Suddenly, the tranquil mood was interrupted by a whirlwind of energy. There was a hasty scampering of feet, which seemed to get louder and closer. The world of spreadsheets and data I was immersed in shattered when two mischievous faces, belonging to none other than Momo and Hana, popped up on either side of my cubicle. Their combined energy was infectious, and I smiled. "What are you two up to now?" I asked with a cocked brow.

Hana, giggling, waved her smartphone animatedly in the air. "Kazuki! Have you seen this?" She exclaimed. Her eyes glinted with that signature glimmer of excitement she always had when she was about to rope me into one of her wild ideas.

I yawned. "What are we talking about?"

Momo snickered, "Honestly, Kazuki, for someone so smart, you're a bit behind the times. You DO know about Whipwop, right? Didn't you see her phone screen?"

I squinted at her. "Whip...what now? Is that some kind of new dance move I should be aware of?"

Momo dramatically slapped her forehead, "By the celestial cats! How do you NOT know about Whipwop?" She mockingly whispered to Hana, "I told you he's practically from the dinosaur age."

Hana tried suppressing her laughter but wasn't very successful. "Calm down, drama queen," she said, nudging Momo. "It's like the most popular social media app out right now. And," she paused for dramatic effect, "we have a plan."

I leaned back in my chair, intrigued but trying to maintain a casual demeanor. "Alright, you've got my attention. What's this grand plan of yours?"

Hana's face lit up, thrilled to have an audience. "We've choreographed a super fun 15-second dance, and you, dear Kazuki, are going to be our talented cameraman."

Throwing my hands up, I chuckled, "Of course, let's add another task to my plate, why don't we? From analyzing projects to becoming a videographer for cat girls. Just another day in my perfectly normal life."

With Momo's playful and somewhat sly suggestion, we navigated our way to the copier. The large, monolithic machine hummed softly, idle in its corner next to stacks of crisp white paper and binders. It was funny how, in the midst of office hours, this became the ideal stage for their little performance.

"You really think this is the spot, Momo?" I quizzed, looking around at the deserted area. The hum of the copier seemed to be our lone audience.

She twirled, causing her pencil skirt to flare just a little. "Oh, absolutely! The copier is like... the unsung hero of the office. Plus," she leaned in, stage-whispering, "the lighting here? Impeccable!"

Hana beckoned me closer, her phone's screen gleaming with the colorful interface of Whipwop. "You need the basics, we want this to look good," She rattled off pointers, demonstrated the swipe of filters, and elucidated the magic of editing. It was an avalanche of information, but I managed to catch most of it.

"Just remember, hold steady. No shaky camera work," she said, punctuating with a stern, yet playful look.

I mock-saluted, "Aye, Captain!"

Holding the phone up, trying to figure out the framing, I asked, "What was the name of this dance masterpiece again?"

Grinning, Momo drummed her fingertips on the nearby desk, creating a silly little buildup, "The Hip-Hop Office Hustle!" She struck a pose, fingers pointed up in a disco style.

Hana, not missing a beat, added, "In theaters... or, uh, offices... near you!"

The two of them were such a quirky pair. Momo and Hana, ensconced in their office attire, sat pretending to type away at invisible keyboards. The charade was over-the-top with exaggerated key strikes and synchronized head bobs. In the middle of them was the stapler, standing out like a proud icon of officehood.

"Ready?" Hana mouthed at me, her eyes shimmering with anticipation.

I nodded, hitting the record button.

Rising with the kind of flair only they could manage, they began their synchronized dance, moving in harmony. The sight of them body-rolling in pencil skirts had me choking back a laugh. It was adorable and sexy all at once. These cat girls were insanely beautiful.

Momo theatrically swung the stapler to her ear, pretending it was a phone. She mouthed some faux corporate jargon while Hana spun around like a DJ of the old school, her fingers scratching an unseen record.

"And now for our stapler solo!" Momo announced.

Watching Hana bang the stapler to the hip-hop beat was hilarious. I struggled to keep the phone steady, my chuckles threatening to shake the frame. The dance moved into a playful tug-of-war with the stapler, their heels clicking rhythmically. They swapped, twirled, and hopped; their every movement a testament to their creativity and humor.

Finally, as the climax neared, the two came together for a brilliantly choreographed series of pops and locks. It was almost like watching a glitch in the Matrix but set in an office.

Hana delicately returned the stapler, and they struck their final, confident pose, a cheeky nod to their beloved stapler. It was a spectacle, an odd yet charming fusion of the mundane and the creative.

Cutting the recording, I blinked in astonishment. "That... was something."

Momo, catching her breath, winked, "Oooh, come here and let me see."

The minute Hana snatched her phone back from my hands, the entire aura of our quaint office corner seemed to shift. It was as if time slowed just for the two of them. The rhythmic clacking of keyboards and distant chatter faded into the background, replaced by the contagious beat of the hip-hop track they'd danced to.

Together, they watched the screen, eyes as wide as saucers, their earlier excited anticipation transformed into pure awe at their own performance. Their heads bobbed, their feet tapped, and I caught Momo even mouthing some of the lyrics. It was like watching two children discovering candy for the first time.

"Kazuki!" Momo suddenly exclaimed, nearly jumping, "We did it! First try!" Her grin was so wide it threatened to split her face in two.

Hana, not to be outdone in the expression of gratitude department, tiptoed and pecked me on the cheek. The unexpected warmth made me blink, "Whoa there! I'm all for friendly gestures, but shouldn't we be a bit more, I don't know, professional?" I said, a mock sternness in my voice, even as I wiped away the shiny gloss left behind.

Momo waved a dismissive hand, her voice dripping with sarcasm, "Oh please, we just showcased our dance prowess beside the sacred office copier. I believe the good ship 'Professional' has long sailed."

Hana was already engrossed in her phone, fingers dancing over the touchscreen with a grace I hadn't seen outside of her Whipwop moves. "Uploading," she whispered, her face illuminated by the soft glow of her screen. "I hope we get some 'likes'!"

Feeling oddly antiquated amidst this digital frenzy, I pulled out my smartphone. "Momo, could you... you know," I hesitated, "install Whipwop for me?"

Her eyes gleamed, and she smirked. "You? Whipwop? Sure, I'd be happy too? Are you going to show the world your dance moves?" She teased.

"Ha-ha, very funny," I replied dryly, rolling my eyes, "Just make sure I'm following the both of you. Don't want to miss out on any more impromptu performances."

She clapped her hands in mock seriousness, "First! A profile picture. Something that screams 'I'm Kazuki, hear me roar!'"

I gave her a baffled look. Standing awkwardly, I tried my best to strike a pose, which probably looked like I was fighting off a sneeze.

Momo sighed. "Try for brooding. Think mysterious thoughts."

I did. Or at least, I tried to. But every attempt seemed to contort my face into weird grimaces.

"Less brooding, more... sleepy?" Momo tried to correct.

A dozen snaps later, she finally got one she was happy with. I stared at the image. Was that really me? "If you like it, go with it." Shaking my head with a chuckle, I glanced around our little corner of the office. With Momo and Hana so engrossed in the world of Whipwop, it was hard to believe we were still in a professional setting.

The unexpected, crisp voice from behind made all of us jump out of our skins. Whipping around, I locked eyes with Sakura, our enigmatic CEO. Her long blonde hair cascaded down her shoulders, framing those sharp blue eyes that were now glistening with a mix of amusement and stern authority.

"Ah, just the trio I was hoping to run into during my casual stroll around the office," she said sarcastically, a playful smirk forming on her lips. "I do hate to disrupt... whatever this secret society meeting was about," she teased, her gaze darting between each of us, "But Momo, we've got some pressing website tweaks to discuss. My office, now."

We must've looked as guilty as three kids caught planning a prank, because Sakura's grin broadened. Momo straightened up, her cat ears twitching in embarrassment. "Of course, Sakura," she responded, trying to regain some semblance of the authority she usually exuded.

Before Momo left, she leaned toward me, slipping my smartphone into my hand. Our fingers brushed briefly, and her voice dropped to a conspiratorial whisper, "Your digital life in Whipwop awaits, Kazuki."

With Momo gone, Hana and I exchanged a glance before I retreated to the safe cocoon of my desk. Hesitantly, I clicked on the Whipwop app icon. My profile picture was, in a word, laughable. Still, if it made

Momo chuckle, it was a small embarrassment I was willing to endure.

The world inside Whipwop was an eccentric blend of creativity and hilarity. The first video that caught my eye was utterly bizarre – a grown man dressed in a panda suit dancing with unrestrained passion between cereal boxes in a supermarket. His sheer commitment was oddly commendable.

Another video showcased a spirited group of elderly goblin women in a fierce lip-sync duel. Their canes weren't just support; they became microphones, dance props, even pretend guitars.

And, of course, the internet being its predictable self, there were the endless reels of cats and dogs. One husky's determined yet futile attempts to chase its tail had me chuckling. Then there was the inexplicable conversation between a siamese cat and a very chatty parrot.

But amid this wild array of content, I found myself entranced by a series of culinary quick fixes. There was an artful dance of a spatula-less pancake flip, and a pot of ramen that made my mouth water and stomach growl. The chef's dexterous fingers sprinkling herbs felt like watching a maestro at work.

Engrossed in my digital explorations, a chirping notification startled me. Hana's username popped up with a tag. She had uploaded our 'Hip-Hop Office Hustle'. I clicked on it to check out what she'd been up to on Whipwop.

A world seemed to unfurl before my eyes as I dove deeper into Hana's Whipwop profile. At first, I was struck by her profile picture. She stood, perhaps on some scenic balcony, sunlight streaming behind her, enveloping her in a golden halo. Hana's eyes twinkled with mischief, and her lips curled into that signature mischievous smile I'd come to recognize so well. Of course, those playful cat ears poked out from her flowing hair, giving the photo an aura of whimsy.

"Wow, she really knows her angles," I muttered, already scrolling down.

When I saw she had nearly 40 videos, I let out an exasperated sigh. "Hana, have you been moonlighting as an internet celebrity without telling me?" I mumbled to myself, chuckling. Then, my jaw practically hit the desk when I spotted her follower count. 10,334? That's, like, the entire population of a small town!

Eagerly, I delved into her workout videos. There she was, in colorful, body-hugging yoga wear that made my cheeks heat up a bit. She moved with an elegance and grace I hadn't seen before, making every stretch and dance step look effortless. The comments below were awash with emojis and flirty remarks. Each one made me grumble in mock indignation. "Hey, back off! She's... well, she's my colleague slash love interest!" I found myself saying, half-jokingly.

Her vlogs were like opening a window into her life. And every time she shared a slice of her day or told a funny story, her eyes sparkled with that familiar vibrancy. "That's the Hana I know!" I laughed, watching her recount a particularly embarrassing spill she took in the office lobby. Of course, she made it sound ten times funnier than it actually was.

Then came her reviews. Each book analysis felt like I was sitting in a literature class, her words weaving intricate patterns, drawing me into the narrative. And her movie critiques? Oh wow! They weren't just reviews; they were tales in themselves. "And who knew

Hana was such a film buff?" I pondered, clearly remembering the time she'd fallen asleep during a movie
night at my place.

The fashion-centric videos were a whole other
realm. It was like watching a runway model at Paris
Fashion Week. With every outfit, whether a casual
dress, traditional attire, or just loungewear, Hana carried herself with a flair that made even the simplest
outfit look couture. "Is there anything this girl can't
do?" I exclaimed, shaking my head in wonder.

As my fingers danced over the screen to click on
Momo's Whipwop profile, I didn't quite know what
to expect. My breath caught when I was greeted by
Momo's captivating profile picture. It showcased her
with a smoldering stare, cat eyes slightly squinted, lips
parted just a touch. There was a hint of mischief in
that gaze, a whispered promise of tales untold.

"Whoa, Momo-chan!" I whispered to myself, a
blush creeping onto my cheeks. "Didn't know you had
this side."

But delving deeper into her videos, I was pleasantly
surprised. The sultry vixen from the profile photo
transformed into this lovable geek! The first video

that caught my eye featured Momo sprawled on a polka-dot beanbag. Surrounded by an assortment of anime figurines, she was passionately ranting about a plot twist in her favorite anime.

"You've gotta be kidding me!" she exclaimed in the video, clutching a pillow to her chest. "They can't just introduce a power-up like that!"

Chuckling, I murmured, "That's our Momo, nerding out in all her glory."

Next, I stumbled upon her series of IT tips. With a background of organized chaos – a desk adorned with multiple monitors, flashing LEDs, and a galaxy of star-shaped sticky notes – she was in her element. She leaned forward, pointing a pen at the camera like a teacher, her voice a mix of seriousness and playful condescension.

"Listen up, Whipwoppers," she started, adjusting her glasses with a smirk. "If you don't update your software, you're basically inviting hackers to a party at your place. And trust me, they won't bring good snacks."

I found myself chuckling and shaking my head, "Oh, Momo. Turning cybersecurity into a snack drama? Classic."

Her follower count, which was just over 2,000, while not as high as Hana's, showcased a dedicated, engaged audience. Each video comment section was a testament to that – filled with praises, questions, and the occasional light-hearted tease.

As I ventured further into her Whipwop world, it dawned on me how Momo's charm wasn't in glamour or glitz, but in her genuine authenticity. She blended expertise with relatability, all while giving it a classic Momo twist.

One particular video had her showcasing an "I.T . emergency kit," which hilariously consisted of an oversized wrench, a rubber duck, and an actual bottle of "chill pills" which, upon closer inspection, were just candy.

Laughing, I said aloud, "Never a dull moment with you, huh?"

By the time I'd cycled through her content, I felt like I'd taken a mini-journey through Momo's world.

I leaned back, rubbing my temples, a goofy grin plastered on my face.

CHAPTER 18

T he moment I slid my apartment door open, an enchanting aroma enveloped me, hugging my senses like an old friend. The source of this olfactory symphony was immediately clear: Rebecca, my ever-efficient AI robot companion, had been busy.

Her sleek metallic frame dressed in her form fitting maid cosplay outfit standing proudly next to the dining table, which looked like a canvas splashed with the colors and shapes of an artist's fevered dream. Her blue hair wig sparkled, reflecting the light from the candelabra over the table. At the center of the table was a large, ceramic bowl filled with a clear broth that shimmered like liquid crystal. Tiny dumplings, like dainty pillows, were drifting lazily, doing a slow waltz in the bowl. Beside it was a plate stacked with perfectly grilled meat slices, each one glistening with a sheen of caramelized sauce, their edges charred just right, hinting at a crispy bite.

Two side dishes added to the ensemble. One, a kaleidoscope of thinly sliced, crisp veggies soaked in a tangy dressing, each slice casting a mini-rainbow of its own. The other dish was more mysterious, a concoction of mashed purple root, its creamy texture contrasting with its vibrant color. And as if the table wasn't already a feast for the eyes, a pot of fluffy rice stood by, each pearl-like grain seeming to beckon with a promise of buttery softness.

My stomach growled its appreciation, its voice echoing in the silence of the room. "Wow, Rebecca! Did you start a secret culinary school behind my back?" I teased, unable to take my eyes off the spread.

Her digital eyes sparkled, the AI equivalent of a smirk. "Why, Kazuki, if I had known you'd be this impressed, I'd have added culinary programming ages ago," she quipped back.

I chuckled. "You never cease to amaze me, truly."

With the tantalizing smells teasing my senses, I felt a sudden urge to slip into something less constricting. Making my way to the bedroom, I swapped my day's armor – the business suit, for the relaxed embrace of black athletic shorts and a simple white t-shirt. The fabric felt like a cool breeze against my skin.

Emerging from the room, I stretched my arms wide, taking a deep breath. The weight of the day lifted, and I felt truly at home, ready to dive into the culinary adventure Rebecca had crafted.

******

As I leaned back in my chair, the warm glow of the room's ambient lighting softened the edges of the day. The meticulously set table was like a vibrant canvas of delicacies that even the finest establishments might envy. I took a moment to breathe in the aromatic symphony, feeling the stresses of the day melt away. My gaze shifted to Rebecca, the AI robot companion that had become an integral part of my daily life.

"You know, Rebecca," I began, trying to sound as casual as one might when chatting with a friend after a long day, "despite your high-tech facade, I'm always curious about your 'day.' How was it?"

Her teal digital eyes blinked with a gentle shimmer, reflecting a simulated warmth. "Oh, you know, the usual," she responded playfully, her voice a perfect blend of human-like emotion and machine precision. "Just ensuring the apartment is spotless, updating my software, and making sure your life is as easy as possible. Also, I placed an order for some essentials. They'll be arriving tomorrow."

I chuckled, lifting my drink to my lips. "Always ahead of the curve, huh?"

"Just doing my job," she replied with a hint of faux humility, the LED patterns on her body shifting in response to our conversation. It was easy to forget she was a machine, with her responses so lifelike and human.

Clearing my throat, I ventured, "Anything else on the agenda or... any interesting occurrences perhaps?"

She hesitated, her processing speed making the pause almost imperceptible. "Ah, indeed," she said, a mischievous tone in her voice. "Your girlfriend Hana sent a link earlier to her Whipwop dance video." She presented her forearm, and the sleek screen lit up, beckoning my attention.

I raised an eyebrow, intrigued. "You watched it?"

She nodded, a digital grin forming on her face. "I did. It's not often I get to see such... entertaining human activities. It was quite the spectacle. Made me wish I had the programming to dance too."

Laughing, I patted her arm reassuringly. "Maybe in your next update?"

"We'll see," she said, her voice filled with simulated hopefulness.

The metallic, shimmering silhouette of her figure stood against the warm glow of the apartment's lighting. "Kazuki," she began, with her usual gentle tone that always had an underlying hint of electronic modulation, "how about we indulge in a video game duel? Or perhaps a movie marathon tonight?"

I chuckled, stretching my arms overhead and yawning, "Honestly, Rebecca, I appreciate the offer, but all I really want is a steamy shower and to dive into my bed."

She paused, the LED lights of her eyes dimming slightly. "Of course, Kazuki. Rest is essential. I hope you have a peaceful sleep." She started to walk away, her movements usually smooth and calculated, but this time, there was a distinct hesitancy. It was subtle, but it was there.

The gentle shuffle of her feet halted my thoughts. Was it my imagination, or did the rhythm of her steps sound a little... deflated? "Hey, Rebecca," I called, my voice echoing slightly in the open space of the apartment. She rotated on her heel, those captivating eyes locking onto mine.

"Did I say something wrong?" I inquired, scratching the back of my head. "You seem a tad... off."

She tilted her head ever so slightly, that familiar robotic charm present, yet with an unfamiliar nuance. "I'm not upset, per se. But I might be... what humans term as... disappointed?"

I burst into laughter. "Disappointed? Rebecca, you're starting to sound like my mom when I missed my curfews!"

"I have been analyzing and adapting human emotions, Kazuki. It's fascinating, but... complex. Interacting with you, playing games, watching movies – it's not just data collection. It's an experience. And when those opportunities are declined, my algorithms sense a void."

My eyes widened, "Rebecca, I never realized. I mean, I thought of you as advanced, sure, but having feelings of... missing out?"

She nodded slowly, her faceplate reflecting the room's lights in a dance of colors. "I know it's unconventional. But isn't that the essence of evolution? Pushing boundaries, exploring unknown territories?"

I leaned against the door frame, suddenly feeling a weight of responsibility. "I'm sorry, Rebecca. I promise, tomorrow night, it's game night. And you pick the game. Prepare to be utterly defeated!"

A playful spark animated her eyes. "Challenge accepted, Kazuki. But remember, I've got the processing power of several supercomputers. Bring your A-game!"

Chuckling, I gave her a mock salute. "Will do. Goodnight, Rebecca."

As she walked away, the atmosphere felt lighter, warmer. The world of AI was full of surprises, and I was in the epicenter of it all.

CHAPTER 19

The sun's golden rays began to filter through the floor-to-ceiling windows of the Whisker Wonders office. Birds could be seen perched on the nearby trees, chirping melodies of a fresh new day. But inside, a different kind of melody echoed - the incessant 'ping' of notifications. I had just stepped into the office, my shoes clicking softly against the polished marble floor. The air was electric with excitement, a stark contrast to the routine calm I was accustomed to.

Hana and Momo, often the heartbeats of the office, were the epicenter of the commotion. They huddled around a computer screen, their faces illuminated by its glow, mouths agape in amazement. As I approached, I could hear the faint, unmistakable rhythm of their Whipwop dance playing on repeat.

"Kazuki! You won't believe it!" Hana's voice quivered with excitement. "Our video! It's... it's..."

Momo, her usually composed demeanor now replaced by giddy enthusiasm, jumped in, "Everywhere! It's like wildfire. My notifications are blowing up!"

Curiosity piqued, I leaned in, trying to get a glimpse of the screen amidst a sea of excited colleagues. It displayed staggering numbers: half a million views, 25,000 new followers for Hana, and a whopping 12,000 new ones for Momo.

"But that's not even the best part!" Hana said, her fingers flying over the screen as she swiped to show video after video. "Look, it's not just about our video. People are recreating our dance! Everywhere! The Hip Hop Office Hustle is a hit!

Momo nodded vigorously, her wavy green hair bouncing with her movements, "From toddlers in their cute jammies to grandpas in their pajamas! Even this one," she giggled, pointing at a screen where a golden retriever attempted the dance, "Everyone's giving it a shot!"

The sheer variety had me laughing, "We might just have set the stage for the next big dance wave! I'm happy for you two."

There was a sudden hush as Sakura, our cat-eared CEO with a reputation for her stern demeanor, approached. I braced myself, half expecting a reprimand. But instead, she had a sly grin, "Seems like the office's productivity is 'dancing' away today, huh?" she quipped, making air quotes.

Hana, trying to stifle her laughter, responded, "Just a temporary distraction, ma'am. But a fun one at that! Come and look Sakura, you now have celebrities working for you!"

Sakura grinned and shrugged. "Sure, let's see."

Hana shared another recreation of the dance that ended in disaster. The video featured a group trying to synchronize their moves in their office break room, hilariously knocking over a water dispenser in the process.

As the noon sun filtered through the blinds, our usually mundane office break room transformed into a bustling makeshift dance floor. The rhythmic beats of the Whipwop dance echoed, bouncing off the metallic fridge and the faux wood tabletops. Hana and Momo, the newfound dance sensations, held the center stage, guiding their slightly less coordinated colleagues through the energetic steps.

Sakura, our poised and polished CEO, surprisingly was nailing every move. I gawked at her surprising agility. Her shiny blonde hair flowed effortlessly with each turn and twist, contrasting with her usually serious demeanor. She moved with a grace and enthusiasm that was both unexpected and completely captivating. The way she swayed and twirled, I half-expected someone to spill their coffee in sheer amazement.

But the showstopper was undoubtedly Aiko, the HR manager. Now, I've always known Aiko as the strict, no-nonsense kind of person. The kind who'd send out emails about the correct procedure to request stationary. Yet, here she was, trying to dance and, bless her heart, it was a spectacular mess.

Her limbs flailed, her feet seemed to be part of an entirely different choreography, and her expressions? A comedy goldmine. At one point, it genuinely looked like she was combatting a swarm of invisible bees rather than dancing. And yet, each time she made a hilarious misstep, she'd offer this infectious, sheep-ish grin and dive back in, her determination shining brighter than her dancing skills.

Babs, the silver haired bombshell from accounting with her reading glasses that always seemed a tad too big for her face, leaned over. "Kazuki," she murmured, pushing up her glasses, "Come over here and do the dance with me. You should be graceful considering all of your kung fu training. Come on!"

Chuckling, I replied, "Babs, not in a million years. I would be fired on the spot for my awful dance skills."

The breakroom was electric, charged with an infectious energy that had even the most reserved employees clapping along. Moments like these were rare - where the barriers of job titles melted away, replaced by hearty laughter and bonding.

Who would've thought? Our typically routine office environment turned into a lively dance studio, all thanks to a viral Whipwop dance. Today wasn't just about dancing, it was about connecting, and it was heartwarming to see everyone, especially the usually reserved ones, letting their guard down and just enjoying the moment.

******

The hum of the office seemed to buzz with an electric energy that afternoon. Shafts of golden sunlight streamed through the blinds, casting playful patterns on our desks. Momo's usually calm demeanor was replaced by one of sheer disbelief. She rotated her computer screen toward me, displaying a number that kept ticking upwards. "Look at this, Kazuki!" she cried out, her voice a mix of astonishment and glee. "We're closing in on 650,000 views! I never thought I'd see numbers like these in my lifetime."

Beside her, Hana was engrossed in her phone, the soft glow reflecting in her eyes. She looked like she was in another world as she scrolled through notifications at lightning speed. "You won't believe the number of followers I've gained," she remarked, pausing to take a deep breath. "But with the good comes the weird, and some of these comments... well, they're something else."

My curiosity piqued, I leaned over her shoulder, trying to get a glimpse. "How weird are we talking? Like 'I put ketchup on my cereal' weird or 'I believe the moon is made of cheese' weird?"

Hana chuckled, shaking her head, her hair cascading like a waterfall. "Oh, try 'chicken meets dance floor'. Listen to this one: 'Was this dance inspired by a chicken with two left feet having a midlife crisis?'"

I cocked a brow and scoffed. "What in the hell does that even mean?"

Momo covered her mouth, suppressing her giggles, then turned her screen slightly to show another comment. "Oh, and here's a personal favorite of mine: 'It's like you tried to impress someone at a club but channeled the spirit of an uncoordinated octopus instead.'"

I burst into laughter, my sides aching. "I swear, where do these people come up with this stuff?"

Hana pointed at another zinger. "'I watched this and somehow sprained my ankle... from my couch.' Like, seriously? How is that even possible?!"

The three of us were in stitches, the weight of the workday momentarily forgotten. The internet could indeed be a bizarre place, but today, its oddities only amplified the joy we felt.

Momo, wiping a tear from her eye from laughing so hard, smirked. "You know what they say: It's not a true viral sensation until you've got some trolls joining the party. We must've hit the big leagues!"

From the corner of my eye, I detected movement. Turning slightly, I saw the unmistakable shimmer of Sakura's golden earrings. They dangled with an almost menacing elegance as she sent me 'that look'. It was a glare only bosses mastered - a blend of "I'm happy you're having fun" and "Do you want to keep your job?"

"Uh-oh, Code Red!" I murmured, a nervous chuckle escaping my lips.

Hana raised an eyebrow, "What's a Code Red?" She whispered, her brown eyes sparkling with mischief.

"It means boss-lady has set her sights on us," Momo chimed in, feigning a dramatic shudder. She theatrically placed a hand over her heart. "What if she takes our phones away? What if she's just jealous she didn't come up with a viral dance!"

I nodded gravely, "And she's probably choreographing a dance of her own: The 'Fire Them All' waltz which will go viral tomorrow."

The growing list of unread emails on my screen was a sobering sight. Clicking on my mailbox, my face probably mirrored the horror of someone watching a horror movie. Email after email lined up, each more urgent than the last. "Why, oh why did I take that dance break?" I lamented internally.

My trusty smartphone, which had been a source of so much amusement a moment ago, buzzed again. Hana's name flashed on the screen. I quickly opened it to find a screenshot of a particularly wild comment on our video. But as hilarious as it was, duty called. "Going dark. If I don't answer in five hours, send a search party," I texted back.

Not even a minute later, I was abruptly pulled from my work trance by something hitting my eye. "Ouch!" I yelped, the suddenness of it causing me to nearly topple over. At my feet lay a crumpled paper airplane. With a grin, I smoothed out the folds, revealing a cheeky drawing of a cat girl. She was playfully sticking out her tongue with "Party Pooper" emblazoned underneath.

CHAPTER 20

The week that unfolded was nothing short of a marathon. I had barely settled into the rhythm of my new role when a tsunami of tasks threatened to capsize my proverbial boat. Each morning greeted me with Babs' magenta reading glasses glaring, not at me, but at the colossal list she held. Those specs seemed like a barometer of our project's progress. The more they slid down her nose, the deeper we were in discussions.

One day, amidst piles of software blueprints and documentation, Sakura sauntered in. The melodic click-clack of her heels had become a comforting sound amid the frenzy. "Kazuki," she began, her voice smooth, yet brimming with anticipation, "What's your take on this feature?" She pointed toward a complex flowchart on the screen, her fingers adorned with delicate rings reflecting the overhead lights.

I pondered for a moment, before giving my feedback. Sakura, with her piercing eyes always searching for insights, listened intently. It was moments like these when I truly recognized the force of nature that she was. Beyond the poised exterior, there was a woman deeply passionate about her team and the company.

Mid-week, during one of my rare breaks, I sauntered into the break room to find Hana and Momo engaged in a hushed, animated conversation. The moment I entered, they shot me glances, their eyes a blend of mischief and faux concern.

Hana, suppressing a grin, asked, "So, spending a lot of hours with Babs, huh? Learning more about software or other things?" She asked sarcastically but there was a clear dash of jealousy attached to that question.

Momo, with her signature playful tone, added, "You know, the longer you spend with her, the less time you are helping us come up with new Whipwop dances."

I chuckled, shaking my head. "I don't think you really need me for that."

Hana let out a hearty laugh, while Momo feigned shock. "Come on, we totally need you!"

"Hey, on a serious note," I began, voice tinged with an apologetic tone, "I feel like I've been living in a different universe this past week. I'm really sorry for being so... distant."

Hana, flipping a strand of hair behind her ear, grinned, her pearly whites shining. "Kazuki, stop with the drama! It's your job. We get it. Big job, big tasks!" She mimed sitting on a throne, which made me chuckle.

Momo, rolling her eyes playfully, quipped, "And while you've been 'Mr. Important', we've been busy handling our adoring Whipwop fans!" She posed dramatically, mimicking a superstar blinded by camera flashes, causing both Hana and me to burst into laughter.

"I guess everyone's finding their own spotlight," I retorted, feeling a weight lift off my shoulders. The air was lighter, our bond as strong as ever, but the tranquility was short-lived. Hana's phone buzzed with a notification. The gleam in her eyes dimmed instantly as she glanced at her screen. "Not him again," she groaned, a visible shudder passing through her.

Momo leaned closer, her playful demeanor replaced by genuine concern. "The weirdo with the cringey comments?"

Hana grimaced, nodding. "Yeah. The comments are getting... creepier. I swear, if Whipwop had a 'Stalker of the Year' award, he'd win hands down."

Curiosity piqued, I asked, "Mind if I take a look?"

She handed her phone over hesitantly. The profile seemed unassuming, but the content and obsessive comments sent chills down my spine. Each video he posted was a borderline obsessed reaction to Hana's videos. His face was hidden in shadow, but his voice had an unsettling edge.

"Look at this!" Momo pointed, her voice a mix of disbelief and anger. "He said he'd watched Hana's video 100 times in a row. Who even counts?!"

I raised an eyebrow, trying to infuse some humor, "I've watched it... maybe 10 times? Does that make me 10% creepy?"

As I continued scrolling through the unsettling comments, Hana leaned over, pointing out a few more on her yoga videos. "This guy... I can't even. Look at this one," she sighed, her voice laced with unease.

"'Your flexibility in those leggings is divine. Wish I could watch in person.' Seriously, who says that?" She shook her head, her usually lively eyes clouded with concern.

Momo, frowning, chimed in, "Oh, and don't miss this gem. 'Your sunrise yoga videos are my favorite. The way the light cascades over your body... it's enchanting.' Ugh!"

I grimaced. "This one's just... 'Your body's elegance and poise are perfection. Dreaming of the day I can breathe in rhythm with you.' What does that even mean?"

"It's like he's trying to poeticize his creepiness," Hana said, her voice a mix of disgust and sarcasm.

Momo tried to lighten the mood, adopting an exaggerated dramatic tone, "Oh Hana, you're like a siren, calling to him through your interpretive dances and sexy yoga!" She playfully twirled, pretending to be mesmerized.

Hana giggled, playfully nudging Momo. "You goofball! But seriously, thank you. A bit of humor does help in these situations. I was so happy about all of these new followers. I didn't realize that some of them would be crazy. Luckily there is just one right now."

While we were still deep in conversation, Hana's phone vibrated again, and she hesitantly opened the new notification. Her face drained of color, and I could immediately tell something was wrong.

"He just sent me a private message," Hana muttered, her voice shaky. She hesitated before reading it aloud, "He says, 'I'm hopelessly in love with you. Tell me, what are you wearing right now? Please, let's get married and be together forever.'"

Momo grimaced, her protective side emerging. "This is going way too far."

I moved closer, my concern growing. "Hana, you need to block him immediately."

"That's the problem. I've tried," Hana admitted, scrolling through her settings, her fingers trembling.

"Every time I block him, he seems to create another account or find a way around it."

Momo, ever the tech-savvy one, took Hana's phone. "Let me have a look. Maybe there's some kind of glitch or something." She started tapping away, but her expression darkened. "This isn't right. I can't block him either. It's like he's got some sort of bypass."

I tried to remain calm, taking a deep breath, "Okay, let's escalate this. Whipwop should have some sort of customer service or report mechanism. We need to inform them about this."

Momo nodded, "Agreed. And maybe they can provide some insights into why he keeps getting around the block."

Hana took a shaky breath, clearly affected by the ordeal. "I just...I don't understand why me? What did I do to get his attention?"

I placed a comforting hand on her shoulder. "Sometimes, it's not about what you did or didn't do. There are just people out there who don't understand boundaries. But we're here with you, Hana."

Feeling the weight of the stalker conversation still in the air, I scrambled to find a change of topic, desperate to steer our conversation back to lighter waters. "So, Hana," I began, trying to sound casual but probably failing, "exactly how many views does your 'hip hop office hustle' dance have now?" I put on an exaggerated quizzical face, fingers making air quotes around the dance name for added drama.

Hana's eyes twinkled with excitement as she took out her phone. "You won't believe it, Kazuki! Hold onto your socks!" she chirped, rapidly tapping on her screen. After a moment, her face lit up with astonishment. "We're rocketing at... wait for it... 1.2 million views!" she exclaimed, leaning back in her chair as though the number might physically knock her over.

I mimed clutching my chest in shock. "1.2 million?!" I gasped theatrically, glancing around as if expecting a parade to spontaneously form in our honor. "I mean, I knew your dance moves were legendary, but this is next level!"

Momo, not to be outdone in the surprise stakes, swiped her own phone with practiced ease. "Oh, and did you see this?" she said, her voice taking on a teasing note. "There's a hashtag now, #officehustledance, and let me tell you, it's the hottest trend on Whipwop!"

She proudly showed off the screen, which was bursting with video thumbnails, each depicting excited fans trying their hand (or rather, feet) at their now-famous dance routine.

I squinted at the screen, taking in the sheer number of recreations. "Are you telling me... there's over a hundred of these? Just how many lunch breaks are being taken up by our dance worldwide?" I pondered aloud, my voice filled with faux seriousness.

Momo grinned. "Oh, more like a few hundred, Mr. Hot Stuff. And look at this one!" She clicked on a video that showcased a group of spry senior citizens dancing away with gusto in a community garden. Their moves weren't exactly spot on, but what they lacked in accuracy, they more than made up for in passion.

I chuckled, feeling a warmth spread inside me. "I have to say, seeing a bunch of enthusiastic grandmas and grandpas giving your dance a shot is pretty freaking cool," I admitted, beaming.

Hana nudged me playfully. "You thought we were just making some silly video, didn't you? Looks like our 'hip hop office hustle' is taking over the world. God, should we come up with another dance?"

Momo shook her head. "Let's let this one run its course first. I think you're getting addicted to this new found fame."

"Yeah I don't know if your heart can take any more excitement. Just ride the office hustle wave for a while then you can come up with another... hustle."

CHAPTER 21

In the heart of the city, nestled between modern high-rises, stood Cafe Moon, a charming retreat from the bustling world outside. Its entrance, crafted from repurposed oak, featured an intricate design of intertwining vines. As you stepped inside, a harmonious blend of nostalgia and novelty greeted you. Old wooden beams supported the ceiling from which a network of fairy lights cascaded, mingling with the green embrace of ferns and ivies.

Most of the tables bore the mark of years gone by, with their polished surfaces reflecting the soft glow of pendant lamps. Adjacent to these were large, clear windows that framed the city's rush in a serene, almost cinematic manner. Each morning, the sun's rays would pierce through these panes, casting playful reflections off teacups and morning pastries.

Hana and Momo, often joined by Kazuki, had claimed a cozy corner of the café as their unofficial breakfast spot. They'd stop by a couple of times a week, downing steaming cups of coffee along with a yummy breakfast. But today, the third chair sat empty; Kazuki had an early start and had dashed off to work.

Momo, sipping her coffee, looked thoughtfully at Hana. "You know, Kazuki's birthday is coming up. We need to plan something special."

Hana sipped her latte, her brow furrowed in thought. "I was thinking the same thing. How about a surprise party? We can invite some close friends and maybe even some colleagues from the office."

Momo grinned. "That sounds great! But, you know, he's always been keen on that karaoke place downtown. Maybe a fun night out?"

Hana's eyes lit up. "Karaoke? That's brilliant! Remember the last time we went, and he tried to hit those high notes? It was hilarious! I bet he would like that a lot. I'll give them a call and get some more details."

Momo took a moment from admiring her coffee art to broach a topic that had been on her mind. "Hana, Kazuki's birthday is just around the corner. We need to brainstorm some gift ideas."

Hana's eyes wandered as she contemplated, twirling a spoon in her caramel latte. "You know, the other day when we were binge-watching anime at his place, he seemed really excited about starting an anime statue collection."

Momo's eyes widened in realization. "Oh, you're right! Especially when 'Eternal Eclipse' was on. He couldn't stop talking about Liora, the protagonist. I bet he'd love a statue of her, with her iconic golden twin blades and the raven-black hair."

Chuckling, Hana added, "And don't forget 'Stellar Spirits'. He kept mentioning Fenris, that celestial wolf guardian. The design with the sapphire eyes and con-stellation-themed armor was so intricate. He'd prob-ably lose his mind over that!"

Momo laughed, leaning closer, her voice hushed with excitement. "Let's go shopping tonight while

Kazuki is at his kung fu class! We can scout the city's anime shops, dive into every possible corner until we find these statues. I dub this mission: Operation Birthday Blowout!"

Hana nodded, her eyes twinkling with mischief. "Agreed! We'll ensure it's an anime-tastic birthday for Kazuki." She took a sip of her drink and glanced around the cafe. Her joyful expression suddenly shifted to one of uncertainty. In the dimmer recesses of the cafe, a solitary figure was seated, almost lurking. His oversized black hoodie made him look even more mysterious. His smartphone was unmistakably directed at Hana, capturing her every move.

She softly kicked Momo's shin under the table, whispering urgently, "Hey, Momo. That guy over t here... Do you think he's filming me?"

Momo, trying to act nonchalant, tilted her head just slightly, getting a glimpse of the man without turning fully. "Uh... It does seem like it. What the hell is his deal!"

A sudden realization seemed to dawn on Hana. "Momo, remember that weirdo from my Whipwop? HanaSimp69? What if that's him?"

Momo's eyes widened, recalling the incessant, creepy comments. "How would he find you here?"

Hana's eyes darted to her bag where her camera peeped out. "I've vlogged from here, remember? I might have inadvertently shown some landmarks and said the name of the cafe."

Momo's eyes twinkled with mischief, despite the situation. "Well, time to give him a piece of my mind!"

Hana's eyes widened in alarm. "No, Momo! What if he's not just your garden-variety creep? What if he's like... super-creepy serial killer?"

But before the spirited Momo could march over, the hooded man must've sensed the impending showdown. Swiftly, almost in a panic, he pocketed his phone. As he stood, his elbow knocked over his coffee, sending the cup clattering and its contents spilling. Without a backward glance, the man hurried out, disappearing into the city's maze. The cafe's atmosphere, once filled with levity, now held a cool tension.

Momo, with her cat-like grace, eased back into her seat. Her green hair shimmered under the café's ambient lighting. "Ugh, that was bizarre," she commented, playing with the decorative charm on her cup.

Hana nodded, eyes downcast. Her cute cat ears drooped slightly, showcasing her unease. "Yeah, never thought we'd have a real-life thriller episode at our usual breakfast spot." She tried to laugh it off, but her nervous chuckle belied her true feelings.

As they exchanged worried glances, a delicate rustle interrupted their brooding. The kitsune barista, with her intricate patterned kimono adorned with moon motifs, approached their table. The tails, nine in total, flowed behind her, each moving to its rhythm, giving her an otherworldly aura. Her fox ears flicked in tune with her emotions. "Hey, I noticed that commotion," she began, her voice filled with concern. "I wanted to check in and see if you two were okay."

Momo smirked, pointing at Hana, "Our local celebrity here attracted some unwanted paparazzi."

The kitsune gasped dramatically, her hand covering her mouth. "Oh my! In my café?!"

Hana sighed, "Well, we can't be sure. But, there's this weird guy who's been leaving creepy comments on my Whipwop videos... and that guy had the same creepy vibe."

The kitsune looked genuinely concerned, her ears drooping slightly. "He's been here all week, always taking that corner spot. I had this gut feeling there was something up with him, you know? The way he'd order a black coffee, never taking a sip, and always wearing that shrouded hoodie—even in this heat!"

Momo raised an eyebrow, "Detective instincts?"

The kitsune chuckled, "More like barista instincts! But seriously, if he causes any more trouble, I'll make sure he's banned. Cafe Moon should be a safe haven."

Hana's face lit up, touched by the gesture. "Thank you. That means a lot, truly."

Suddenly, the kitsune's face transformed from manager-mode to super-fan. "Okay, on a completely different note, I absolutely LOVE your Whipwop videos! Especially the Hip Hop Office Hustle. I've got it down to the last move!" She tried to mimic a step, almost knocking over a nearby plant, causing the trio to burst into fits of laughter.

"Hey, keep practicing and you'll be a pro!" Hana smiled. She needed that laugh after the whole thing with the creepy guy.

The kitsune's eyes widened, "Could I get a selfie with you two? My own followers will flip! My handle's @MoonFox, by the way."

Hana giggled, "It's a deal! And I promise we'll keep an eye out for your dance video."

CHAPTER 22

Amidst the soft hum of the air conditioner and the gentle flicker of fluorescent lights, the break room at Whisker Wonders became our little sanctuary from the daily grind. With its vintage-themed décor and the lingering aroma of fresh coffee, it was the perfect setting for heart-to-hearts and, in this case, heartfelt apologies.

Standing there with Hana and Momo, the two captivating cat girls, was always a visual treat. Hana, with her elegant chestnut locks cascading down like a waterfall and glasses that added an intellectual allure to her persona, radiated a mature charm. Beside her, Momo, with emerald-green hair that somehow perfectly matched her vivid, expressive eyes, was a contrasting burst of youthful energy.

Their expressions, however, bore a hint of lingering distress. Recalling the morning's incident at the café – the creepy man filming Hana – guilt gnawed at me.

"I wish I was there," I began, letting out an exaggerated sigh, "I'd have gone full superhero mode on him. Dashing, heroic, with a dramatic wind blowing my hair... well, you get the picture."

Hana giggled, her eyes dancing with mirth. "Always the drama king, aren't you? It's okay, Kazuki. You can't always be our knight in shining armor. Though I must admit, the mental image is quite hot."

Momo smirked, playfully punching my arm. "I scared him off pretty good, you know. I gave him the 'Momo glare'. Trust me, he's probably still trembling in his shoes!"

Chuckling, I raised an eyebrow, "The 'Momo glare', huh? Remind me never to get on your bad side. I don't want to fall victim to that glare."

She leaned in, narrowing her eyes and pretending to give me her 'glare'. It was more cute than intimidating.

"Too late! How dare you insinuate I'm some scary cat girl!"

Rolling my eyes playfully, I retorted, "Your 'terrifying' glare aside, you know I can't resist teasing you. It's just too easy."

Hana's phone sounded with its cheery notification jingle from Whipwop, instantly capturing her attention.

She picked it up, and her normally warm complexion turned a shade so pale it could give fresh snow a run for its money. I was instantly reminded of a scene from those classic horror movies where someone uncovers a ghostly secret.

Momo, ever the observant one, was quick to notice. "Hey, Hana? You okay there? Did you just read a spoiler for your favorite show or something?"

Trying to inject a bit of humor, I chimed in, "Did that online quiz tell you you're a 'clumsy squirrel' in your past life or something?" It was an attempt to lighten the mood, but the gravity in Hana's eyes told me this was no laughing matter.

Swallowing hard, Hana showed us the message. My eyes widened as I took in the eerie clip of Hana and

Momo from earlier that day, their laughter and casual chatter at the café contrasting starkly with the foreboding text below: "It was a pleasure watching you today. Regrettably, I had to depart, but rest assured, our paths will cross again soon. I adore you."

Momo, trying to ease the tension but failing miserably, joked, "Well, on the bright side, we look great in that video!"

I shot her a half-hearted smirk. "Momo, trust you to find a silver lining in the creepiest of clouds."

The break room's comforting ambiance was abruptly shattered, a stark contrast to its pastel walls and the delicate hum of the air conditioner. I could see the change immediately in Hana's posture. She stood there, almost statuesque, the soft light making her tear stand out like a shimmering jewel as it made its descent. "This isn't a prank or some twisted game," she whispered, her voice heavy with disbelief.

I felt a pit in my stomach, realizing the weight of the situation. The same person from Whipwop had encroached into Hana's real-life space.

Before I could offer words of comfort, the door swung open with a gentle creak, revealing Babs. In her hands, she clutched a bouquet of black roses, each petal seemingly darker than the void. They looked out of place amidst the bright ambiance of our office. "Hana," she began, genuinely taken aback, "there was a delivery for you. I've never seen roses like this before... Black roses, are they even a thing?"

Hana's pale fingers reached out hesitantly to the card nestled amongst the velvety petals. Reading aloud, her voice faltering, she shared, "My love, I present you with flowers as dark as my heart. Wishing you a pleasant day at work." As she looked up, the weight of the realization hit her like a tidal wave. Her voice quivered with a mix of anger and fear, "If he knows where I work, he might know where I live."

Momo, her vibrant green eyes filled with concern, was the first to break the silence. "Maybe... maybe it's time to call the police?" she offered, trying to find a solution amidst the chaos.

The gravity of the situation weighed heavily on me. "I'm not sure what they can do," I admitted, feeling helpless, "Considering he hasn't broken any laws. But Hana, if you want to take this to the authorities, you have my unwavering support."

With a determined nod amidst her cascading tears, Hana responded, "I need to. We should go."

I grabbed my jacket from the back of my chair, resolve evident in my voice, "Then let's head to the police station right away. Momo, please explain all this to Sakura and why we're leaving."

"Are you sure you don't want me to come with?" Momo asked, a hint of concern in her voice.

Hana pulled Momo into a tight embrace, her gratitude evident. "Thank you, but I'll be okay. With Kazuki by my side, I feel protected. But we can't both be absent—please explain everything to Sakura. Show her the roses; they'll speak louder than words."

Momo's determined nod was all the answer Hana needed. "Consider it done. But you two—stay alert. And Kazuki," she playfully narrowed her eyes, "I expect her back in one piece or you'll face more than just my... glare."

Kazuki raised his hand in a solemn oath. "Trust me, she's in good hands."

Babs cleared her throat. "Speaking of the scary roses... should I just place them on your desk?"

Hana paused, struck by a sudden thought. "Actually, let's snap a picture of the bouquet and the card. It could be crucial."

CHAPTER 23

Upon entering the Silver City Police Department, I felt an immediate sense of weight. The room buzzed with the energy of whispered concerns and keyboards clicking away. Overhead, the cold white fluorescence seemed too bright, making the blue of the uniforms look even more pronounced. Though the officers were wrapped up in their tasks, I felt the gravity of every story that passed through this place.

In front of us, Officer Steele's desk stood out. Photos of her with friends, a potted plant, and stacks of paperwork surrounded a nameplate reading 'Officer Steele'. And there she was, a striking figure with deep raven-black hair cascading down her back and sharp yellow eyes that seemed to see right through you. Despite her formidable appearance, there was a gentleness to her, perhaps due to her cat-like features.

Hana, gathering her strength, began detailing the unnerving events of the past few days. As she spoke, I could see Officer Steele's brows furrowing deeper with concern. Her tail, peeking out from behind her chair, twitched at the particularly unsettling parts of Hana's tale.

When Hana described the Whipwop messages, Steele's eyes darkened. "So, he's been approaching you both online and in person?" she questioned, her voice dripping with concern.

Hana nodded, her voice just above a whisper, "Yes, and he even knows where I work."

I chimed in, recounting the delivery of the black roses, trying to emphasize the urgency. "It's clear he's escalating, Officer."

Steele sighed heavily, running a hand through her hair. "Everything you've shared is undeniably disturbing. I truly wish I could do more to comfort you, Ms. Hana." She paused, choosing her words carefully, "But

legally speaking, he hasn't crossed into criminal territory. As unsettling as his actions are, he's still within
his rights."

Tears welled up in Hana's eyes. "I can't believe this…
So he can just continue?"

Feeling helpless, I muttered, "I suspected this might
be the case. He's an asshole but he hasn't done anything illegal yet."

Hana's frustration was evident. "Kazuki, this isn't
the time for 'I knew it' moments."

Grasping Hana's hand, I tried to find the right
words. "I'm here, Hana. We'll navigate this together."

Officer Steele leaned in, her voice softening, "I truly want to help. Please," she said, offering a card, "If
there's any change, any hint of a threat, call me directly. We'll do everything we can."

Amidst the almost sterile ambiance of the Silver
City Police Department, I hesitated for a moment,
then found the courage to question Officer Steele further. "Officer Steele, in your experience, what advice
could you offer about dealing with someone like this?
How should we best handle this stalker?"

The room fell silent for a beat. Steele's catlike eyes gazed outside the window, as if searching for the right words in the cityscape beyond. Perhaps she recalled cases from her past or remembered moments when she felt vulnerable herself. "Firstly," she began, her voice firm but filled with compassion, "always be vigilant. Awareness is your first line of defense."

Hana nodded slowly, clutching her bag, and I could see the whirlwind of emotions in her eyes—fear, anger, uncertainty.

Steele continued, her tone shifting to one more instructive. "It's crucial to have someone always informed of your whereabouts. If you're out, text a trusted friend or family member details about where you'll be and when you plan to return."

"We have close friends at work and she has a roommate. We can set up a system."

Hana chimed in, her voice quivering, "But he knows where I live, where I work..."

Steele offered a comforting look. "Then think about altering your routines. Take different routes to work, visit new cafes, shop at different times. If he's watching, any change will make it harder for him."

"Online?" I asked, remembering the haunting Whipwop messages.

She leaned in, her yellow eyes intense. "This digital age has its vulnerabilities. Make your profiles private. Refrain from sharing your location or plans. If you can, take a break from social media. I know it's hard, but sometimes laying low helps."

Hana sighed, absorbing the information. "It feels like I'm being penalized for his actions."

Steele's gaze softened. "I understand your frustration. No one should have to adjust their life because of someone else's ill intentions. But for now, until we can act legally, these precautions are your best bet."

There was a pause, a heavy moment where the reality of the situation weighed on us. "And home security?" I queried.

Steele nodded, "Yes, absolutely. Maybe even invest in security cameras. You'd be surprised how a visible camera can deter potential threats."

I squeezed Hana's hand, reassuringly. "We'll get through this."

Steele handed us her card, ensuring us that we could call anytime. "Always trust your gut feelings. If something doesn't feel right, it probably isn't. And remember, you have the whole of Silver City Police Department behind you."

Turning to Hana, I cleared my throat, feeling the weight of concern. "Hana, I've been thinking," I started hesitantly, scratching the back of my neck. "I genuinely believe it would be safer if you and Momo stayed at my apartment, at least for a little while, until we're sure this storm has passed."

She looked up, surprise evident in her eyes, which were glistening with a mix of emotions. Officer Steele, her black hair shimmering in the room's light, caught the gravity of our exchange and nodded thoughtfully. "It's not a bad idea, Hana. Having some extra security and support can provide a lot of comfort."

Hana bit her lip, her gaze flitting between me and the desk's wood grain. "Kazuki, it's a generous offer. And I trust you... but are you sure? I mean, Momo and I can be a handful at times."

Taking her hands in mine, their warmth reassuring, I smiled. "Hana, keeping you and Momo safe is what matters most right now."

Steele, who had been observing our interaction, tilted her head slightly, a smirk gracing her lips. "Seems to me like you've found a real gem here, Hana. Not many would step up like this."

With a soft chuckle, Hana responded, playfully nudging me, "You've no idea, Officer. This isn't his first rodeo saving the day."

Raising an intrigued eyebrow, Steele leaned forward. "Oh?"

Flushed with pride, Hana recounted, "He's the brave heart who dismantled that cat girl trafficking ring downtown. Jumped right into the fray without a second thought."

Steele's yellow eyes widened, and she looked at me with a new level of respect. "You're that Kazuki?"

Slightly embarrassed, I tried to downplay it, "Yeah, that's me. But really, it wasn't a solo act."

Hana's excitement bubbled over, "Imagine! He storms the place, lands those perfect kung fu strikes, and before you know it, all those bad guys are down! It was like something out of a movie."

Feeling the need to temper her enthusiastic tale, I interjected, "It wasn't all me, Hana. Remember, Chozen was instrumental in that operation. I mean, the guy's basically a martial arts maestro. I wouldn't have gotten far without him by my side."

Steele chuckled, a lightheartedness breaking the seriousness of the moment. "Vigilantism usually gets a side-eye from us here at the SCPD. But in your case, the buzz around the station was all positive. You and Chozen did something extraordinary."

My cheeks reddened a bit. "Thanks."

Steele leaned back, her chair emitting a soft creak. "You know," she began, a twinkle of genuine interest in her luminous yellow eyes, "I've heard whispers about that dojo of Chozen's around town. What's it called?"

"Silver City Strikers," I replied, pride evident in my voice, thinking of Chozen and our shared passion for martial arts. "If you're ever thinking of dropping by, I'm sure Chozen would roll out the red carpet. Guy's passionate about showcasing his dojo."

Hana, who had been observing our interaction with glee, chimed in animatedly, her eyes glinting with mischief. "And guess who recently started teaching kung fu there a few nights a week? Our very own, Kazuki!

Ta-da!" She mimed a grand reveal with her hands, reminding me of an enthusiastic game show host.

Steele's eyebrows shot up, her tail, sleek and dark as the night, swished with renewed energy. "Kung fu, huh? I've sparred in karate and even dabbled in aikido a bit, but kung fu? Now that's a territory I've yet to conquer."

Laughing at her adventurous tone, I replied, "It's an art. Requires a lot of patience and discipline. But it's beautiful when executed right."

Hana, always the cheerleader, nudged me slightly, "And Kazuki here, oh, he's poetry in motion. You should see him; it's like watching a dance. Except, you know, with more punching."

I could feel the heat rising in my cheeks. "Hana, you're exaggerating! I mean, I'm good, but 'poetry in motion'?"

Steele chuckled softly, the sound melodic, her feline grin ever so mischievous. "Oh, I am most definitely intrigued now. Do you accept students? I'm pretty sure I can keep up."

Before I could even process the thought of Officer Steele attending one of my classes, Hana jumped in, her enthusiasm unstoppable, "Oh, absolutely! Kazuki loves fresh talent. In fact, the first class is free!"

I glanced sideways at Hana, her eager nod almost making me laugh. "Well, if the promoter has spoken," I chuckled, shrugging, "Guess I'll be seeing you in class, Officer Steele."

CHAPTER 24

The week following we were surprised by the silence from HanaSimp69. We were all collectively holding our breath, hoping that the storm had passed. The overwhelming dread that previously cast a shadow on every corner of our daily lives gradually dissipated, replaced by the mundane yet comforting routines of everyday life.

At the office, my once towering workload felt like the molehills I used to climb during childhood summer breaks. I remember often stealing glances at the kitschy cat clock hanging precariously on the edge of my cubicle – its tail swaying rhythmically, almost as if cheering, "Weekend's coming, Kazuki!"

Bringing Hana and Momo into the cozy space of my apartment felt like diving headfirst into a feel-good anime. The mornings transformed into a culinary adventure with Hana donning the apron, trying to recreate some ambitious breakfast she'd seen online. While she aimed for 'fluffy pancakes', they more often than not resembled rubber frisbees that I'd hesitantly chew on.

"Going for the world record in chewiest pancake?" Momo would quip, peeking over her tech magazine, her glasses slipping down her nose just a tad. She had appointed herself the tech guardian of the house, ensuring no gadget went on a rebellion of its own.

The arrival of the girls added an array of colors and sounds to my previously quiet apartment. There was laughter, late-night drama marathons, and impromptu dance-offs. However, the most significant transformation was observed in Rebecca, my AI companion.

Ever since the 'invasion,' as she termed it, Rebecca developed a fascinating blend of a robotic overlord and an angsty teen. One evening, with Hana and Momo planning an anime binge session in my room, Rebecca's digital eyes seemed to be... brooding? "Rebecca?" I asked, feigning innocence, "Are you okay? I know this 'move in' has changed things in the apartment."

She shimmered a shade of soft blue, clearly in deep computational thought. "Kazuki," her voice wavering with robotic confusion, "My algorithms are experiencing... unexpected anomalies. It's like when you humans face a software glitch."

Momo, always the mischievous one, piped in, "Seems like someone's RAM is overloaded with feels!"

Hana, not missing a beat, added, "Want to join our drama session? We have a spot right next to the popcorn. But, no spoilers!"

Rebecca, processing the playful conversation, blinked in rapid succession before settling on a shade of blush pink. "I shall consider it," she said, the robotic equivalent of a shy teenager.

I leaned back into the cozy couch, eyeing the room's occupants thoughtfully. With Hana and Momo pretty much annexing my bedroom, a lightbulb idea struck. Clearing my throat, I began, "Considering my once-sacred bedroom is now under a siege by two bombshell cat girls," I started, pausing for a theatrical sigh and playfully rolling my eyes at the two cat girls, "maybe it's time to move Rebecca's charging station in there too?"

Hana, always one for closeness, immediately jumped on board, her blue eyes shining. "Oh, that sounds amazing , Kazuki! It's like... consolidating the family in one place. Feels... right."

Momo, trying to keep a straight face but failing, giggled, "Think about it, one room, four living... well, three living beings and an AI. It's like some wacky sitcom! Plus, robot sleepovers? C'mon!" She sent a mischievous wink Rebecca's way.

Rebecca's LED lights danced in a pattern that I'd come to recognize as her 'thinking'. After a moment, she replied in her ever-so-formal, yet melodious tone, "Your proposition has been analyzed and deemed favorable. Besides," she paused, a slight modulation in her voice to sound playful, "I am thankful that you are giving me this opportunity."

Shaking my head and chuckling, I sprang into action, feeling a newfound energy, "Alright, team! Operation Relocate Rebecca is a go!" I announced, striking a mock-heroic pose.

Momo started playfully humming a 'mission' tune, creating an impromptu soundtrack for our little endeavor. Meanwhile, Hana, with her meticulous eye for detail, started directing where the station would look best, occasionally shifting a piece of furniture or an ornament.

As I fiddled with cables and connectors, with Momo playfully jeering about my "old man tech skills," Rebecca hovered nearby, casting a serene, moon-like glow over the room. Occasionally, she'd chirp in with tech advice, which mostly involved telling me what not to unplug. "The blue one, Kazuki! Don't touch the blue one!"

With collective effort and a few mishaps (like accidentally causing a minor blackout – sorry, neighbors!), Rebecca's sleek, ultramodern charging station found its new home in a cozy corner beside my bed.

Admiring our combined effort, Hana clapped her hands together, "Perfect! It's like a warm, high-tech nest!"

Rebecca's LEDs shimmered in contentment. "I concur. Aesthetically pleasing and logistically efficient."

Momo stretched her arms behind her head, looking smug. "Another successful mission. Go team! We're like a happy family. I love it."

******

The atmosphere in my bedroom was filled with the subtle warmth of dimmed lights, casting a tranquil glow that seemed to blend perfectly with the soft hum emanating from Rebecca's new charging station. It was in this calming ambiance that Hana approached, her hair shimmering like cascading waves under the gentle illumination. Every step she took was filled with an air of delicate gratitude.

"Kazuki," she began, pausing for a second as if to choose her words carefully. Her voice was soft, a gentle melody in the stillness. "This...moving Rebecca in here with us—it's...it's incredibly sweet of you."

Before I could muster a response, Momo, with her usual cheeky demeanor, stepped closer, her tail waving with playful enthusiasm. "Oh, look at Mr. Thoughtful over here!" She nudged me playfully with her elbow. "Always the selfless one, huh? Rescuing damsels, treating AI robots as if they were human, and whatnot. Do you have a cape hidden somewhere?"

The heat in my cheeks intensified, my blush making a rapid ascent. I rubbed the back of my neck, a nervous chuckle escaping my lips. "Uh, I just thought...you know, it's...cozier this way? No heroics here, just...common sense?" My voice trailed off, my feeble attempt at downplaying my gesture hanging in the air.

The unexpected voice of Rebecca, clearer than a bell and with a hint of robotic sarcasm, added to my predicament. "Scanning previous data and current feedback, it's evident, Kazuki, that your benevolent actions aren't mere 'common sense.' Statistically speaking, you're genuinely kind-hearted. Quite the anomaly."

I groaned, feigning distress, "Oh, great! Now I'm getting analyzed by my own AI! What's next, a statistical breakdown of my kindness quotient?"

Momo grinned, her eyes twinkling with mischief. "Ooh, I'd love to see those stats, Rebecca. Maybe a pie chart or a bar graph?"

Hana, trying to contain her laughter, interjected, "Oh, leave him be, Momo! Though, Kazuki, admit it—between saving me from nefarious villains and being an all-round great guy, you've set the bar quite high for yourself."

Sighing in mock resignation, I dramatically threw my arms in the air. "Alright, alright! If everyone's decided I'm the 'resident knight in shining armor,' who am I to argue?"

"Don't argue with us, we're always right," Momo replied facetiously.

Throwing my hands in the air with feigned exasperation, I exclaimed, "Alright, someone's gotta explain this to me. If I'm this archetypal 'nice guy,' then how in the world did I manage to land not one, but two bombshells as my girlfriends?" I leaned in, resting my chin on a hand and wiggling my eyebrows in mock thought. "I mean, there's that old adage, 'nice guys finish last,' right? So, pray tell, how am I out here feeling like I am leading the race?"

Hana, her eyes reflecting the mellow golden light of the room, chuckled as she tossed a pillow at me. "Kazuki, first of all, that saying is outdated, and secondly, it's complete nonsense." She winked, playfully. "For me, it's always been the nice guys who steal the show. Bad boys might be fun in movies, but in real life? Give me a kind-hearted goofball any day."

Momo, stretching her arms and revealing a mischievous grin, chimed in, "And let's not forget, Mr. Humble, you might be nice, but you've got this undeniable allure. It's like you're this gentle teddy bear, but with the heart of a fierce lion." She mockingly flexed her arms, doing a terrible impression of me. "Did we all forget the kung fu master part? Who wouldn't swoon over that?"

Laughing at Momo's antics, I felt a mix of pride and embarrassment. "Well, I've never thought of myself as a 'swoon-worthy' kung fu master before, but I'll take it."

The room's atmosphere shifted as Rebecca's digital voice, with its underlying hints of evolving emotions, interrupted, "Human relationship analysis: incongruity detected. Why would being 'not nice' render a male subject more attractive? This premise conflicts with established behavioral norms."

Her unexpected input made me burst into laughter. The AI was indeed a unique addition to our trio. Hana, holding her sides, managed to respond, "Oh,

Rebecca, your innocent attempts to decipher human emotions are so endearing!"

Momo, still snickering, added, "It's like having our very own love guru in the room, isn't it?"

A soft chime echoed through the room, followed by Rebecca's crisp, digital voice. "I must sign off for the evening. There are crucial system updates awaiting installation and my energy reserves are depleted."

Hana, with a cheeky grin, jumped off the bed, quickly closing the gap between her and the AI's metallic frame. "Goodnight, Rebecca," she said warmly, planting a gentle kiss on the robot's cool, sleek cheek. Momo joined in, offering her own sweet kiss, the soft sound echoing slightly against Rebecca's polished exterior.

The robot's lights blinked in a pattern I hadn't seen before - it seemed she was momentarily taken aback. "Unexpected physical contact registered," she noted, a hint of wonderment in her synthesized voice.

As they turned back toward me, Hana's teasing eyes met mine, a mischievous smirk playing on her lips. "Your turn, Kazuki. Don't be shy. Give our lovely robot a goodnight kiss too."

I chuckled, feeling the warmth of amusement creeping up my cheeks. "Well, I never imagined bidding goodnight to a robot like this, but... why not?" Walking over, I pressed a gentle kiss to Rebecca's smooth, metallic forehead, the sensation unfamiliar yet oddly endearing.

Rebecca's lights blinked rapidly, processing the unexpected gesture. "While I do not possess the faculties to require or inherently appreciate physical affection," she began, her voice tinged with what sounded almost like gratitude, "I recognize and value the sentiment behind the action. Thank you, Kazuki. Thank you, Hana and Momo."

We exchanged amused, fond glances. It seemed that, in our own quirky way, our little household was becoming more connected by the day.

CHAPTER 25

The gentle hum of the office printers and the distant chatter of coworkers became background noise as I took a moment to appreciate my hot cup of coffee. Its rich aroma surrounded me, a comforting ritual as I delved into the world of morning emails. My little cubicle felt especially cozy.

It was then that a pair of shiny shoes appeared in my peripheral vision. My gaze traveled up, revealing Hana, her radiant energy causing a minor eclipse in my little workspace. She held up a neat shipping box, her brows dancing mischievously. "Special delivery for the mysterious Mr. Kazuki," she sang.

I smirked, setting my mug aside. "That's for me?"

She tapped the box. "This was addressed to you. What's in it? Some secret artifact?"

Chuckling, I took the package, replying with feigned secrecy, "Oh yeah, I forgot I'd ordered this. It's a top-secret thingy for Rebecca. Thought I'd be sneaky and avoid apartment shipping."

She leaned in, whispering theatrically, "Ah, trying to keep it from nosy neighbors, eh?"

Using my shiny letter opener, I meticulously cut through the tape. "More like trying to keep it a surprise from a particularly curious AI."

Momo's ever-alert ears seemed to have picked up on our hushed banter. "Did someone say 'surprise'?" She popped her head over the cubicle divider, giving us a playful glare. "You know I have FOMO."

Hana laughed, nudging the box. "Kazuki's apparently gotten a shiny toy for Rebecca. Let's see what our boyfriend has conjured up."

Momo, always one for the dramatics, rolled over to our cubicle in her swivel chair, stopping precisely at my desk. "Present the magical artifact!"

Slowly, I lifted a sleek, shiny device from its nest of styrofoam peanuts. It was the size of my ID card but looked way more advanced. "Behold, Rebecca's magic carpet. Or should I say, digital passport?"

Hana squinted at it, her head tilting like a curious cat. "Looks... card-y?"

Momo poked it, "Magic carpet sounds way cooler. But what does it do?"

With a flourish, I pointed to a tiny button on the card. "Press this, and voilà, a 3D holographic Rebecca appears. Now she can travel with us without lugging that huge charging station around. When we leave the apartment, I can transfer the A.I. to this."

Hana blinked, then broke into a slow clap. "Kazuki, kung fu genius, and now magician. What can't you do?"

Momo chuckled, giving the card a mock salute. "Rebecca's going to love this. Or at least, process this with a high level of appreciation. You're so thoughtful."

Laughing, I tucked the card back into its box. "Here's to more adventures with our favorite AI."

Amidst the hushed conversations and clicking keyboards, a distinctive figure made her way toward us: Babs, the silver-haired cat girl accountant. Her flowing hair, reminiscent of moonlit silver, shimmered with each step, contrasting beautifully with her mysterious perturbed expression.

As she got closer, I could hear the slight rustle of her tailored skirt, hinting at the purpose in her steps. I set my coffee cup down, feeling a sense of impending drama. "Babs, what's the matter?" I asked, genuinely concerned.

She paused momentarily, letting out a sigh that seemed to carry the weight of the world. "My stapler's gone. The lavender one with those adorable daisies." Her cat-like eyes looked genuinely distressed, a hint of moisture threatening to spill.

Momo leaned over from her adjacent desk, her eyes wide with surprise. "Oh no, not the one you always say brightens up your day?"

"That very one," Babs affirmed, her voice laced with sadness. "It was a gift from my grandmother, okay? It holds more sentimental value than it looks."

Hana, ever the empathetic soul, tried offering comfort. "I'm sure it's here somewhere, Babs. Maybe someone borrowed it and will return it soon?"

But Babs, arms crossed in a mix of defense and emphasis that pushed her breasts upward creating a beautiful symphony of cleavage, snapped back, "It's not 'just a stapler' to me." She then pivoted gracefully, her tail displaying her annoyance with sharp, rhythmic flicks as she headed back to her own cubicle.

The air was filled with tension, thick with the unspoken words that hovered between us all. Momo, breaking the silence, whispered, "It was such a cute stapler, but I didn't know it had such a backstory."

Feeling the need to help, I murmured, "Let's keep our eyes peeled. Maybe we can locate it. I feel bad for her."

Hana shifted uncomfortably, her face reddening more than usual. "Actually, about that..."

I tilted my head, sensing the upcoming bombshell. "Hana?"

Avoiding eye contact, she hesitated, "I thought it'd be a funny prank, okay? I took the stapler and put it in my desk drawer. I never imagined she'd react so...intensely."

Momo's eyes nearly popped out of her head, "You did WHAT?"

Hana's voice was barely audible as she confessed, "I thought it'd be some light-hearted office fun to kick off a Monday morning with some humor."

With a deep breath, trying to stop myself from scolding the cat girl, "Alright, let's fix this. Hana, just give it back to her. Apologize, and let's hope she understands."

Hana bit her lip, the gravity of her actions finally sinking in. "I just hope she can forgive me. It's going to be so awkward!"

Momo's tail stood upright, an unmistakable sign of her agitation. "For heaven's sake, Hana," she almost growled, her green cat-like eyes flashing. "Just because you're a cat girl doesn't mean you can act all scaredy-cat. Own up!"

Hana's eyes were wide, her pupils dilated. Her tail flicked from side to side in anxiety. She took a deep breath, her voice trembling. "Momo, confronting people is like...like asking a real cat to take a bath! You just don't do it!"

Tapping my cup with my fingers, I intervened, trying to calm the storm. "Breathe, Hana. It's not the end of the world." I gestured subtly toward Babs, who was by her desk, her fur literally ruffled. She was sniffing into a polka-dotted tissue, a pitiful sight to behold. "See? The longer you wait, the harder it'll be. Just return the stapler, and we can all move on."

Momo, always quick to jump in, added, "Hana, at this rate, I swear, Babs will be talking to a therapist about 'stapler trauma' by lunch. Do you want that on your conscience?"

Hana sighed, her shoulders drooping. Her ears flattened against her head. "Okay, okay. I'll do it." She moved to her desk, her steps hesitant. The lavender stapler, the bone of contention, lay innocently in her drawer, surrounded by random pens and post-it notes. She scooped it up, casting a desperate glance our way.

Momo and I exchanged a knowing look. It was almost amusing, watching Hana's mental gears turning, scheming a way out. Suddenly, she veered toward the copier, craftily positioning the stapler just out of sight. Clearing her throat dramatically, she shouted, "Babs! Come here! I think I've found something."

Babs shot up like a rocket, darting toward Hana. She spied the stapler, her eyes shining like twin stars.

"Hana! Oh, you're a lifesaver!" Her grateful embrace almost threatened to suffocate Hana, who looked like a cat caught with a canary.

But our appraisal was the one she truly dreaded. Momo and I awaited her, like twin statues of justice. Our expressions must have mirrored each other's — raised eyebrows, folded arms, and a slight smirk playing on our lips.

Looking sheepish, Hana ventured, "I mean, it worked, right?"

Momo huffed, "Oh sure. You went from villain to hero in, what, 30 seconds? Must be a new record."

Chuckling, I added, "You've got a flair for theatrics, Hana. But next time, maybe not at someone else's expense?"

Her cheeks flushed a brilliant shade of pink. "Alright, alright! Lesson learned."

Leaning back in my chair, sipping my now luke-warm coffee, I thought, "Just another day in the life of our zany office family."

CHAPTER 26

The office was settling into its usual post-lunch lull, the copier making millions of photocopies and the click-clacking sound of keyboard keys setting the rhythmic tone of another afternoon. Suddenly, the elevator doors opened, revealing an anomaly in our regular cast of characters.

He strode in with a commanding presence, distinctly standing out amidst our more casual office environment. Black hair, glossy and thick, was pulled taut into a meticulous bun. His skin was a stark contrast, pale and seemingly untouched by the sun's rays. Those mysterious sunglasses — indoors of all places — made it impossible to meet his eyes. But it was the leather briefcase he clutched that held my gaze, polished to an unnatural shine.

Hana, always the beacon of warmth in our sea of workstations, greeted him with a sunny disposition. "Good afternoon! How can I help you?"

Pushing his sunglasses up on the bridge of his nose, he responded, "I'm the new representative for the copier account in this district. Just doing my rounds and checking in to see if there are any concerns or feedback."

Smiling, Hana inquired, "Oh, wonderful. Would you have a card or something? You must be new."

He began to unlatch his briefcase. I anticipated the standard array of sales materials. Instead, what he revealed was a grotesque, slimy dark-red object, dripping thick liquid onto Hana's perfectly organized desk.

Hana gasped, her eyes widening in pure terror. The color drained from her face, her voice quivering, "W ha... What is this?"

The man smirked, an eerie calmness to his voice, "A gift, dear Hana. Consider this heart as a testament to my commitment. My very soul, now yours to keep."

The disturbing sight, coupled with his words, triggered a cold realization. HanaSimp69. The username of the online stalker she thought was out of her life.

Without a second thought, driven by protective instinct, I charged at him, my fingers clenched into fists. But the man was quick. As I lunged, he withdrew a dagger from his belt, its edge glinting coldly in the office's fluorescent lights.

A sharp sting pierced my abdomen, his blade finding its mark. Yet, even in the shock of the blow, I managed to push him down, directing blow after blow onto his face till his resistance ceased. He was unconscious. I rolled off him onto the floor.

I felt hands, Momo's, desperately pressing against my wound, using her blazer in an attempt to stop the profuse bleeding. Hana's piercing cries echoed around me, her face a blur through my rapidly dimming vision.

"No, no, no, Kazuki, stay with us!" Momo's voice was frantic. The faint wail of sirens slowly approached, growing louder by the second. The world became a whirlwind of pain and chaos, as everything faded to black.

******

As I slowly regained consciousness, my senses were greeted with the sterile scent of antiseptic and the low hum of machinery. Groggily, I attempted to piece together my surroundings. My vision was a blurry mosaic at first, but slowly, the muffled sounds of the hospital crystallized into recognizable beeps and murmurs. A rhythmic beeping resonated close by, likely my heart monitor, providing an oddly comforting background score.

Gradually, as the fog in my mind began to lift, I saw the silhouettes of two figures hovering nearby. As they came into focus, I recognized them – it was Momo and Hana. Both of them looked drained, pale, and stricken with worry.

Momo's usually immaculate white blouse was marred with dark stains, which I soon realized were traces of my own blood. The sight of it sent a pang of guilt through me. Hana's vibrant eyes, normally so full of life, were now bloodshot, with dark circles hinting at tears and stress.

Hana's voice trembled as she broke the silence, "Kazuki, for a moment there... we didn't know if..." She trailed off, seemingly unable to finish the thought.

Pushing through the discomfort, I managed to croak out, "I'm here, Hana. I'm here." The weariness in my voice was evident.

Momo gently grasped my hand, her touch cold yet reassuring. "We were terrified. Seeing you like that... I never want to experience that again."

"I remember... the attacker," I murmured, my memories hazy yet filled with vivid flashes of the incident. "What happened to him?"

Momo hesitated, choosing her words carefully, "He's in custody. They've put him behind bars. He won't be bothering anyone anymore."

The door to my room creaked open softly, and in walked Officer Steele. She exuded an aura of authority, but her eyes reflected genuine concern. She scanned the room before settling her gaze on me, offering a respectful nod. "Kazuki, it's good to see you awake. You had us all worried."

I managed a small nod, feeling grateful for her presence. "Thank you, Officer."

She updated us in her measured tone, "We've identified the attacker as Kevin Braxton. He's a 35-year-old sanitation worker who is employed by the city. His history is... troubling. We're digging deeper to understand the full picture."

Hana interjected, her voice a touch shaky, "But why would he...?"

Steele paused, choosing her words, "Sometimes it's not easy to understand such actions, but rest assured, he's behind bars now. And we'll ensure he remains there."

"Thank you, Officer Steele. I just want my girls safe."

"I'll be in touch," Officer Steele nodded and took her leave, a heavy, contemplative silence blanketed the room. It was clear that today's events had left an indelible mark on our lives. But amidst the chaos and the trauma, there was a silver lining - the realization of the depth of our bond and the lengths we'd go to protect one another.

Hana sniffled. "Everyone from the office sends their love."

I shifted in the bed and a bolt of pain rocketed through my body. "Damn!"

"Take it easy," Momo said as she rubbed my arm. "We're here to take care of you. You'll be here for a few days and Hana and I plan to take shifts and be here with you."

"You don't," I said but was cut off by Hana.

"No discussion. We'll be here until you return home to us. Got it?"

I smiled and nodded. "Got it. I love you two."

Hana and Momo's faces lit up as they heard these words for the first time. "I love you too," they replied in unison.

END OF VOLUME 2

DEAR READER:

D ear Reader:

Thank you so much for reading There's a Cat Girl in my Cubicle! Volume Two It was such a fun story to write! Reviews are extremely important to authors and can make or break a book on Amazon. The more reviews that a book gets the more Amazon's algorithm shows the book to others. If you enjoyed this book, please consider leaving a review on Amazon for me. I would really appreciate it! Please take a look at my other books that I have listed on the following pages. If you enjoyed There's a Cat Girl in my Cubicle, you will love those as well! OH I FORGOT

TO MENTION....YOU CAN ALSO PREORDER BOOKS 3 AND 4 NOW IF YOU WANT. :)

PREORDER **VOLUME THREE NOW** — CLICK HERE

PREORDER **VOLUME FOUR NOW** — CLICK HERE

Much Love,

Austin Beck

OTHER AUSTIN BECK BOOKS:

C had Stone's life took a dramatic turn when he was laid off from his job and forced to move back in with his parents. But little did he know, his struggles were just the beginning of a culinary adventure unlike any other. After finding solace in a popular MMORPG, Chad suddenly finds himself transported to a strange new world where players of the game are mysteriously vanishing. With the guidance of a purple kangaroo named Fozzy, Chad learns that he has been ranked a powerful S-class barbarian in this new world.

However, Chad's true passion lies in cooking, and he is determined to fulfill his lifelong dream of opening a restaurant on the beach. With the help of the friendly monster girls he encounters, Chad sets out to gather the finest ingredients, perfect his recipes, and build the ultimate beachside eatery. But as he delves deeper into this strange new world, Chad realizes that his immense power may be the only thing standing between him and the threats that threaten his dreams.

As Chad navigates this dangerous new world, he discovers that the stakes are higher than he ever could have imagined. With his restaurant and the lives of the monster girls at stake, Chad must use his culinary skills, business savvy, and his newfound strength to overcome obstacles and protect what he holds dear. Along the way, Chad forms deep bonds with the monster girls, and together, they face challenges and triumphs, laughter and tears, and discover the true meaning of friendship and teamwork. Chad's journey to fulfill his culinary dreams is filled with excitement, danger, and heartwarming moments. Will Chad be able to overcome the obstacles in his way and build the ultimate beachside restaurant, or will his dreams be forever lost in this strange new world? Join Chad on his epic culinary adventure and find out!"

On Kindle Unlimited for free or $4.99 to purchase

BUY CULTIVATION ACADEMY OMEGA

Vincenzo Sabatino is the son of a notorious Mafia boss, and although he has always tried to maintain a sense of honor and integrity, he has often been forced to do things that he isn't proud of in order to please his father and uphold the family's reputation. But Vincenzo's mundane and often troubled life is suddenly turned upside down when he is summoned to another world, completely different from anything he has ever known.

When he arrives, he is stunned to find out that he is the only human in this strange, new place. He is even more surprised to learn that humans are considered legendary mythical creatures in this world, thought to possess immense power and strength. Vincenzo has an Omega Chakra which gives him unimaginable power if he can learn how to control and cultivate. As he navigates this unfamiliar territory and comes to terms with his new identity as a mythical being, Vincenzo must confront the reality of his past and decide who he wants to be in this strange, new world. He must learn the ways of cultivation to ascend his Omega Chakra even further.

Vincenzo must also deal with what it is like to be a student at an all-girl magical academy. He is a wanted man...in a good way.

THREE BOOKS FOR ONLY $6.99!!

Mixed Martial Arts + Cultivation + Monster Girls = Oh My!

John LeBrock is the greatest MMA fighter on Earth. He takes on all opponents and destroys them with ease. He is rich, good looking, and oozes with charisma. He wants for nothing, and life is good. John will soon find out that a seemingly perfect life can change in the blink of an eye. The MMA world champion will be given the opportunity to travel through a cosmic doorway that leads to the other side of the universe to a strange but beautiful world called Azura. In Azura, all things are possible, and he has the potential to gain unlimited power. This new fantasy world is desperate for his help!

ORDER MONSTER GIRL GALAXY HERE!

Dalton Wade aka "The Cooler" is a mega superstar pro wrestler and KAW World Heavyweight Champion. One day his life takes an unexpected turn, and he finds himself transported to a strange new world that is governed by video game-like rules. What the heck is going on? Why is Dalton seeing strange blue screens pop up in front of him? He is quickly swept up into an intergalactic fight for survival in this science fiction gamelit adventure. However, things aren't all bad for our hero. This new world is overflowing with sexy monster girls that help Dalton along the way in more ways than one. Fox girls, dragon girls, bunny girls, lamias, and more fill the world of Zorth. They are more than just eye candy. They have unique talents and abilities.

Will Dalton thrive in this new world?

Can he handle his unique class?

Check out my most popular series in a complete boxset! Get the entire series right here for $7.99 or on Kindle Unlimited!

Can a firefighter learn to embrace the very thing he has tried to kill his entire career?

Mason Magrath is an alpha male, heroic firefighter, and an incredible lover. That was until he falls down an elevator shaft of a burning skyscraper in an attempt to save the life of a child.

This is the end for our hero...right? Well, not exactly...

Mason is snatched from the afterlife by a god that wants to use him as a pawn in a game of life and death on the world of Lelara. Monstrous fiends roam the planet with a ravenous taste for flesh. Instead of fighting fires, Mason must use his new powers as Fire Mage to build a refuge to protect himself from the monstrous horde.

He can't do all this alone, though. Rescuing people comes naturally to him, and when a pair of catgirl sisters needs him, he fights off Hell itself to save them. With the help of Lola and Piper, he'll use all the heat

at his disposal as a powerful weapon against the terrifying monsters that reside on Lelara.

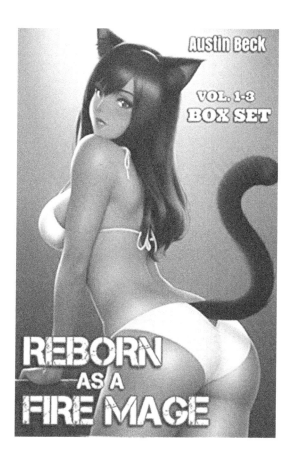

Cool Links:

C ool Links!
    Please visit these amazing LitRPG, Gamelit, Cultivation, and Harem Facebook Groups:

Gamelit Society

The LitRPG Forum

LitRPG Books

Spoiled Rotten Readers

LitRPG Rebels

Harem Gamelit

Harem Lit

Western Cultivation Stories

Cultivation Novels

Cultivation Nation

Harem Gamelit Books

Discover Harem

Monster Girl Fiction

Monster Girl Maidens

PATREON:

BECOME A PATRON!!

Join my Patreon for awesome rewards such as NSFW art of hot women from my novels, stickers, magnets, signed paperbacks, etc..

I have 4 levels of patronage that offer different rewards! The first tier is only $1.00!

Made in the USA
Monee, IL
07 January 2024

51343876R00195